It was all Jesse's fault.

Jesse and that damned hot mouth of his.

And now Tania's life was being shaken up. Shaken up for the first time since she'd consciously pulled her emotions out of the game, sealing them away.

She'd never lost herself before—lost the ability to think clearly. To function. For more than just a split second when Jesse kissed her at the door, her mind had gone blank and her body had grown hot. As for the longing...

Well, she just didn't do that. Didn't long for anyone. And yet...

Jesse had made her long.

Made her want...

Dear Reader,

Welcome back for the fourth installment of THE DOCTORS PULASKI. I cannot begin to tell you the memories working on this series brings back for me. I grew up in New York City—Queens specifically—and worked in a building that looked out on Radio City Music Hall. At lunchtime, I would walk the very streets I'm writing about now. And while the hospital where my dedicated doctors work is fictional, the Diamond District in the first chapter is very, very real.

Many a lunch hour was spent looking into windows along that route and sighing. The engagement ring my now-husband bought me came from one of those shops. After the purchase, he brought the ring right over because he was afraid of losing it, which is how I came to be engaged on the twenty-second floor of what was then The Equitable Building. You'll soon see why all this brings back fond memories for me.

In reading about Tatiana and Jesse, I hope their story sparks you into creating fond memories of your own.

As always, I thank you for reading and with all my heart, I wish you someone to love who loves you back.

Marie Ferrarella

MARIE FERRARELLA

A Doctor's Secret

Silhouette®

Romantic

SUSPENSE

SILHOUETTE BOOKS

ISBN-13: 978-0-373-27573-1
ISBN-10:   0-373-27573-0

A DOCTOR'S SECRET

Visit Silhouette Books at www.eHarlequin.com

Printed in U.S.A.

MARIE FERRARELLA

This *USA TODAY* bestselling and RITA® Award-winning author has written more than 150 novels for Silhouette Books, some under the name Marie Nicole. Her romances are beloved by fans worldwide. Readers can visit her Web site at www.marieferrarella.com.

To Misiu and Marek, and growing up in New York City.
Love, Marysia

Chapter 1

"Stop, thief!"

When he looked back at it later, Jesse Steele would have to say those words had ultimately changed his life. Had he not heard them, he probably would have never met her.

It was an overcast Manhattan late spring morning and he was worried about rain. That, and making the meeting on time.

One moment he was taking a shortcut through New York's famous Diamond District. He had to hurry because New York's more famous traffic was making it impossible for him to get back to his office in time for the one o'clock meeting with the senior partners of the architectural firm of Bryce, Newcomb and Tuttle. The next moment he was breaking into a run, charging down the crowded sidewalk and then tackling a rather upscale but guilty-looking man running from the scene.

The rather elderly distinguished man who had uttered the cry stood in the narrow doorway that led to his small, exclusive shop on the second floor. Dressed in dark slacks, a white suit and a black vest, the unique ties of a prayer shawl peeked out from beneath the bottom of the vest. A black, hand-sewn yarmulke completed the picture.

The blood from the cut on the old man's cheek was a startling contrast to his somber clothing. He swayed slightly as he clutched at the doorjamb, but the anger on his face was fierce.

All this Jesse had taken in within half a heartbeat. While heads turned toward the man in the doorway and several women yelled a protest as the object of the old man's cries barreled down the long city block, Jesse sprang into action. Using the prowess that had gotten him a football scholarship and seen him handily through his four years at NYU, he flew after the thief.

Throwing his weight forward, Jesse grabbed the man by the waist. They both went down on the concrete less than a foot shy of the gutter.

Frantic to get away, the robber fought and kicked with a fierce determination that only made Jesse angrier. Nothing got to him as quickly as someone trying to take advantage of someone else. The robber was young, strong and well-built. The man in the doorway looked as if he could easily blow away in a stiff breeze.

"Let go of me, you bastard!" the thief shouted, his arms flailing wildly as he tried to beat Jesse off.

Still struggling, the thief cracked him across the side of his head with what turned out to be a toy gun. He'd used it to intimidate the store owner. Jesse's grip on the man tightened and he brought the thief down, straddling him to keep him in place.

The bag the thief clutched when he fled the store flew out of his hand and spilled. Diamonds appeared on the concrete, creating their own rainbows in the sparse available light.

Suddenly the people in the immediate area came to life, converging on the two struggling men, their attention collectively focused on the brilliant booty displayed for them to see.

Jesse was on his feet instantly, holding on to the thief's arm and jerking him up in his wake.

"Don't even think about it," Jesse ordered one man who was close to him. The latter was bending to scoop up some of the bounty.

Jesse's harsh voice, added to his six-two stature, succeeded in keeping the man honest and the rest of the crowd at bay.

The man in the doorway took out a handkerchief to dab at his wound as he hurried over to Jesse. Shock and surprise registered on his bewhiskered face.

"Thank you, young man. Thank you," he called even before he reached Jesse. "My name is Isaac Epstein and you have done me a great service."

The thief was squirming next to Jesse, doing his best to get out of his grasp.

"Let me go!" the man ordered. When Jesse merely glared at him, the thief's indignation retreated. He became supplicant and meek. "Look, this was all a big mistake. A big, stupid mistake. I won't—"

Jesse had no desire to listen to anything the man had

to say. Anyone who would try to rob an old man was worthless—worse than dirt in his opinion.

"Shut your mouth," he advised evenly. "You'll get a chance to explain your side of it to the police."

The man's eyes widened even more, bulging like marbles. "The police?" he echoed. "But I—"

The sound of approaching sirens abruptly halted the thief's protest. But not his attempts to get away. He tugged mightily, getting nowhere rather quickly.

Jesse's smile was as steely as his last name. His fingers tighten around the thief's arm, squeezing it as he continued to hold the man in place.

"You're not going anywhere," he told the thief coldly. Jesse looked down at his light gray suit. There was a tear at the knee and what looked to be an oil stain across the other leg, sustained when they'd wrestled on the ground next to the subway grating. *Damn it.* Jesse swallowed a curse. "But when this is over, you are going to buy me a new suit."

What the would-be thief said in response was enough to offend several of the people watching the minidrama.

Jesse jerked him up, squeezing even harder as he held his arm. The man yelped.

"You say anything like that again," Jesse growled, "and I guarantee that you'll be picking up your teeth from the sidewalk."

If there was a retort coming, it disappeared as the sirens grew louder. Two squad cars and an ambulance arrived almost at the same time, one practically tailing the other.

The thief whimpered.

* * *

Tatania Pulaski loved being a doctor, or more accurately, loved being a resident. Tania was in her fourth year, that much closer to being able to hang up a shingle if she so desired. She loved everything about her duties, even the grosser aspects of it. Very little of what she dealt with at Patience Memorial Hospital fazed her.

Even so, she took nothing about her journey or her ultimate goal for granted. She, like her three older sisters and her one younger one, had paid her dues and was acutely aware of every inch of the long, hard, bumpy road it had taken to get here. She knew the sacrifices her parents had made and the contributions each of her older sisters had made. It was an unspoken rule: the older always helped the younger. It was just the way things were.

Although her heart was focused on becoming a spinal surgeon, there was no task Tania wasn't willing to do if the occasion came up. The only thing she didn't like were the rare moments that other doctors lived for.

A lull in the activity.

She didn't like lulls. Lulls caused her to think and, eventually, to remember. To remember no matter how hard she tried not to, no matter how often she forced herself to count her blessings first.

She had a great many of those and counting always took a while. She had a supportive family, parents and sisters who cared about her. Even her brother-in-law and the two men who, very shortly, were going to become part of the family were all nice guys.

On top of that, she was becoming what she'd always dreamed of being ever since Sasha, her oldest sister, had announced she was going to be a doctor. The revelation gladdened the heart of her father and, most of all, her mother.

All Tania had to do was to take in the scene that long-ago afternoon and that made up her mind for her. She was going to be a doctor. She, too, was going to save the world one patient at a time. The fact that Natalya and Kady followed in Sasha's footsteps only made her resolve that much stronger that she was going to be a doctor, too.

There'd only been one dark incident to cast a stain on her life, one in comparison to the multitude of blessings, and yet the shadow of that one stain managed to cast itself over everything, blackening her life like a bottle of ink marring a pristine white sheet.

One stain had caused all the happiness to slip into abeyance.

She tried, more for her family's sake than her own, to put it behind her. To forget. But forgetting for more than a few minutes at a time was next to impossible. The incident lived with her every day, shadowing her. The memory of it found her when she was at ease and assaulted her mind, making her remember. Making her suffer through it.

Especially in her dreams.

Trying to block it out of her mind was the reason why she'd eagerly volunteered to work in the emergency room every time the area was shorthanded. Ninety-nine times out of a hundred, the E.R. was crowded with patients, all seeking immediate help. The atmosphere was nothing short of frantic and hectic. And nothing made her happier than being there. She was forced to concentrate on procedures, on patients who needed her help.

And while she concentrated on that, the cold, hard

reality of what had happened to her that one horrible evening was pushed into the background.

For the time being.

This particular morning the bedlam that was called the E.R. seemed especially acute. A trauma bay was no sooner emptied than someone else was brought in to fill it. She'd been on duty for close to twelve hours, on her second "second wind" and had cleared over thirty-one cases before she stopped counting.

Tania felt dead on her feet and there were still several hours to go until her second shift was finally over.

Be careful what you wish for.

It wasn't an old Polish saying, like the ones her mother was so fond of quoting, but it certainly did fit the occasion.

She was just erasing the newest case she'd discharged, which meant she was up for the next patient, when another fourth-year resident, Debbie Dominguez, tugged on the sleeve of her lab coat.

When Tania glanced in her direction, the dark-haired woman pointed to the rear doors that just sprang open. The look in Debbie's eyes was envious.

"Boy, some people have all the luck." She referred to the fact that Tania was up for the patient being brought in by two ambulance attendants.

Strapped to the gurney was a tall, muscular man in what appeared to be a disheveled, gray suit. The patient's hair was several shades darker than her own blond hair and he didn't exactly look happy to be there.

Behind him were two more gurneys, one with an older, somber-dressed man and the second with a rather vocal patient. The latter had a police escort in addition to the two attendants bringing him in.

"I don't need a doctor," the man in the gray suit on the first gurney protested. "Really, all I need is just to get cleaned up."

The older man on the second gurney seemed noticeably concerned. "Please, young man, you need stitches. I know these things. I will take care of everything. The hospital, everything," he promised with zeal. "But you need to have medical attention."

The head ambulance attendant began rattling off the first man's vitals. Tania listened with one ear while giving the man on the first gurney a swift once-over. As far as patients went, they didn't usually come this exceptionally good-looking. While distancing herself, Tania could still see why Debbie had been so interested. Any more interested and the woman would have been salivating.

When her patient struggled to get off the gurney, Tania placed her hand on his shoulder.

"Listen to the man," she advised, nodding toward the second gurney. "He's right. Besides, if you put on another suit, you're just going to wind up getting blood on it unless I stitch you up."

Turning his head in her direction, Jesse's protest died in his throat. His eyes swept over her and he had to admit he did like what he saw.

"You're my doctor?"

Rounding the corner to the trauma bays, feeling as if she was at the head of a wagon train, Tania grinned in response to the appreciative note in the man's voice. "I'm your doctor."

Jesse settled back against the gurney. "I guess maybe I'll take those stitches."

"Good choice." She looked at the attendants still guiding the gurney. "Put him in trauma bay one."

"I thought you said—" Jesse craned his neck to keep sight of her.

"Be right there," she promised.

Moving to the second gurney, she nodded at the older man. "Looks like you'll be getting the group rate for stitches," she commented, examining the gash on the man's cheek.

Isaac shrugged, as if this was nothing new to him. "Never mind me, young lady, make sure that he's all right." Wrapping his long, thin fingers around a black bag he was clutching, with his other hand he pointed in the general direction that Jesse had gone in. "He's a hero, you know."

Tania glanced over her shoulder even though by now the gurney had been tucked away into the trauma bay.

"No, I didn't know." She smiled at the man. "So that's what one looks like," she murmured, playing along with the older man. She took a step back, getting out of the gurney's way, then pointed toward another area. "Put this one in trauma bay three," she instructed the attendants.

"Treat him well, Doctor," Isaac called to her as he was wheeled away. "Anything he needs, I will take care of."

"He'll have the best of care," she promised before she turned her attention to the last gurney. The attendant closest to her gave her the patient's particulars. The latter looked far from happy, but it was a toss-up as to who was more disgruntled, the patient or his police escort.

The man on the last gurney struggled against his restraints. "It's a mistake, I tell you. The old guy must've slipped the bag in my pocket when I was leaving his store."

"Now why would he do that?" she asked. She'd come across all kinds in the E.R. and this was just another odd case to add to the list.

"I don't know. Maybe he wanted to pull some insurance scam. Who knows? Do I look like a thief to you?" he demanded hotly, indicating his clothing. Tania had to admit, except for the tear in the jacket, it looked like a high-end suit. "I'm going to sue that ape in the gray suit for battery and if you don't want to be included, you'd better uncuff me!" he growled, yanking at the handcuff that tethered him to the gurney's railing. "You hear me?" he demanded. "I want out of here."

"No more than we want you gone, I'm sure," Tania replied evenly. "But we can't have you bleeding all over the place now, can we?" she asked sweetly. Glancing at the board over the front desk to see which room had been cleared, she saw a recent erasure. "Put him in trauma bay number four." She pointed in the general direction, since she didn't recognize these attendants. Tania spared the third patient one last glance. "Someone'll be along to talk to you in a minute."

"Not soon enough for us," one of the patrolmen complained. He shook his head wearily as he followed in his partner's wake. "It's the heat," he confided to Tania as he walked by. "It makes the crazies come out."

She smiled. "So does the rain." Tania signaled over toward the nurses' station. "Elaine, take the gentleman's information in trauma bay three."

"What about one?"

"I'll handle that myself."

Elaine nodded, a knowing smile on her lips. "I thought you might." Picking up a clipboard, she walked into trauma bay three.

Armed with a fresh clipboard and the appropriate forms, Tania went to trauma room one.

The moment she walked in, she could feel the man's restlessness. Not the patient type, she thought, amused. Well, they had that in common.

While waiting for someone to come in, Jesse had taken off his jacket in an effort not to get it any more wrinkled than it already was. He wasn't altogether sure why he did that. There was no saving the pants and without the pants, the jacket was just an extraneous piece of clothing.

Habit was responsible for that, he supposed. Habit ingrained in him since childhood, when every dime counted and no amount was allowed to be frivolously squandered or misspent. Stretching money had been close to a religion for his parents. They'd taken a small amount and somehow managed to create a life for themselves and for him.

He twisted around when he heard someone enter the room.

And smiled when he saw who it was.

"Hi." She extended her hand to him. "I'm Dr. Pulaski. And you are…?"

"Jesse Steele."

Succinct, powerful. It fit him, she thought, trying not to notice how his muscles strained against his light blue shirt.

"Well, Jesse Steele, I'm afraid there's some paperwork waiting for you at the nurses' station, but first, let's see the extent of your injuries."

"It's nothing, really," he protested. The woman was drop-dead gorgeous and in another time and place, he would have liked to have lingered. But hospitals made him uneasy and, in any event, he definitely had somewhere else he needed to be.

"The blood on the side of your head says differently," she replied cheerfully. With swift, competent fingers, she did her exam. "I need you to take off your watch. I think you have a cut there."

"It's just a scratch."

"Potato, po-ta-to, I still have to see it." He took off his watch and set it aside on the nearby counter, then held his wrist up for her to see. "Okay, that's a scratch," she asserted. "You win that round. However—" she indicated his head "—that definitely needs attending to. Which means I get to play doctor."

She smiled brightly as she crossed toward the sink. "So—" she turned on the faucet and quickly washed her hands "—I hear that you're a hero."

"Not really," he answered with a mild shrug. Heroes were people who laid their lives on the line every day. Cops, firefighters, soldiers. Not him. "I was just in the right place at the right time. Or…" His lips gave way to a hint of a smile. "Taking it from the thief's point of view, in the wrong place at the wrong time."

"Do you always do that?" she asked, looking at him as she slipped on a pair of plastic gloves. "Look at everything from both sides?"

Crossing back to him, she gingerly examined the gash at his temple more closely.

He tried not to wince. She could feel him tensing ever so slightly despite her light touch.

"Occupational habit," he replied through clenched teeth.

Taking a cotton swab, she disinfected the wound. He took in a bracing breath. "You're a psychiatrist? By the way, you can breathe now."

He exhaled, then laughed at her guess. "No, I'm an architect. I'm used to looking at everything from *every* side," he added before she could ask for more of an explanation.

"Never thought of it that way," she confessed.

It was good to keep a patient distracted, especially when she was about to run a needle and suture through his scalp. The best way to do that was to keep him talking about something else.

A quick examination showed her that the bruises were superficial, but the gash at his temple was definitely going to require a few stitches.

"Well, aside from a couple of tender spots that are going to turn into blacks and blues—and purples— before the end of the day," she warned him, "you do have a gash on your right temple. I'm afraid I'm going to have to take a couple of stitches." He looked as if he was going to demur, so she quickly added, "But don't worry, they won't be noticeable. You'll be just as handsome as ever once it heals."

"I don't need stitches, it's just a cut." He shrugged it off. "So, I guess that's it," he said, beginning to get off the examination table.

She put her hands on his upper torso to keep him from going any farther. For a little thing, he noted, she possessed an awful lot of strength.

"No, it's *not* a cut. That thing on the inside of your

wrist is a cut. That—" she pointed to his temple "—is a full-fledged gash that needs help in closing up. That's where I come in," she added cheerfully. "You're not worried about a little needle, are you?"

"No, I'm worried about a big meeting." He blew out a breath, annoyed now. If he'd stayed in the taxi, he wouldn't have gotten into this altercation. But then, he reminded himself, the old man would have lost his sack of diamonds. "The one I was going to when this happened."

"Important?" Tania pulled over the suture tray and, taking a stool on rollers, made herself comfortable beside the gurney. "The meeting," she added in case he'd lost the thread of the conversation.

Right now, her patient was eyeing the surgical tray like a person who would have preferred to have been miles away from where he was.

"To me." He watched as she prepared to sew him up. From where he sat, the needle and suture was one and the same entity. He'd never been fond of needles. Jesse sat perfectly still as she numbed the area. "I was supposed to do a presentation. That was why I was cutting across the Diamond District," he added. Then explained, "Because the traffic wasn't moving and I needed to be there in a hurry."

She nodded, her eyes on her work. "Lucky for that man that you did." When he stopped talking, Tania momentarily raised her eyes to his face. Amusement curved her mouth. "I could write you a note, say you were saving a nice old man from a big bully," she teased. "It'd be on the hospital letterhead if that helps."

"No, I already called them to say I'd be late. They weren't happy about it, but they understood."

Her eyes were back on the gash just beneath his hairline. He had nice hair, Tania caught herself thinking. Something stirred within her and she banked it down. There'd be no more wild rides, she told herself sternly. They always led nowhere.

"Sound like nice bosses."

"They are. For the most part," he qualified in case she thought he had it too easy. Nothing could have been further from the truth. "What they are is fair."

"So," she said in a soothing voice, taking the first tiny stitch, "tell me exactly what you did to become a hero."

Chapter 2

Tania heard the man on the gurney draw in his breath as she pierced the skin just above his temple. He sat as rigid as a soldier in formation.

Not bad, she thought. She'd had big, brawny patients who had passed out the very moment she'd brought needle to skin.

"It's nothing, really," Jesse said in response to her question as she slowly drew the needle through. He was aware of a vague pinching sensation and knew he was in for a much bigger headache later, when the topical anesthetic wore off.

Tania smiled to herself. Modesty was always a nice quality. It was also very rare in men who looked as good as Jesse Steele did. There was something about women throwing themselves at their feet that gave handsome men heads that barely fit through regulation-size doorways.

She kept her eyes on her work. "The man in trauma room three seems to think you're the closest thing he'd seen to a guardian angel. And the man in trauma bay four thinks you're the devil incarnate, so my guess is that you must have done something."

He was probably going to have to give a statement and maybe show up in court, as well, if it came to that. No good deed went unpunished, Jesse thought.

Still, he did feel good about having saved the old man's diamonds. "I tackled him."

The doctor arched an eyebrow. He found it very sexy. "Excuse me?"

"The guy with the police escort," he clarified. "I tackled him."

"Why?" she asked.

His response had been immediate. There hadn't been even a moment's hesitation. "Because the old man yelled 'stop thief,'" he told her and then, before she asked, he added, "and the guy in the suit was the only one running away from him."

She could see why the old man had sounded so grateful. "That was pretty brave of you," she acknowledged. "Most people would have looked the other way or pretended not to hear."

He couldn't do that, couldn't look away or count the cracks in the sidewalk when someone needed help. He hadn't been raised that way, wouldn't have been able to live with himself if he'd just walked on. "I don't like thieves."

"Most of us don't," she agreed, humor curving her lips. And then she paused for a second to scrutinize him. There was more to this man than just looks, she decided. "Sounds like it's personal." Because her father had been and her new brother-in-law still was involved with the police force, she guessed, "Is someone in your family in law enforcement?"

He had meant to stop with just the first word, but somehow the rest just slipped out. She was extremely easy to talk to. "No. Someone in my family was robbed."

Something about the way her patient said it made her look at him again, her needle poised for a third tiny stitch. "Who?"

"My parents."

Tania felt her heart tighten in empathy. "What happened?"

Her patient blew out a breath and was quiet for so long, she thought he'd decided not to answer. Which was his right. She was prying.

But just as she completed the last stitch, he said, "My parents ran a small mom-and-pop-type grocery store in Brooklyn. We lived right above it. One night some thug came in and robbed them. When he tried to steal my mother's wedding ring, my father pushed him away. The thug shot him point-blank and ran. My mother got to keep her wedding ring, the thug got seventy-three dollars in cash, and my father died." His voice was stony. He could still remember hearing the shot and wondering what it was. He was home that night, struggling with his math homework and planning on asking his father for help. He never did do his math homework that night.

Tania cut the black thread and felt numb. When he mentioned his parents, she could envision her own, Magda and Josef, being in that situation. Granted, her father was a retired police detective, but, judging from the way Jesse's jaw had tightened, the underlying emotional ties were the same.

She lightly placed her hand on his arm. "I'm very sorry."

He nodded, trying to put distance between himself and the memory of that night. The memory of flying down the stairs and bursting into the store, only to see his father on the floor, not breathing, blood everywhere. His mother sobbing. Funny how it still cut so deep, even after all these years.

Jesse cleared his throat. He could feel the passage growing smaller, threatening to choke him. "Yeah, well, that happened a long time ago. I was thirteen at the time."

Sympathy filled her. "Must have been rough, growing up without a father."

She didn't know what she would have done without hers. Especially after the incident. It was her father who'd broken through the stone wall she'd built up around herself rock by rock. Her father who'd held her hand throughout the ordeal and who'd given her the courage to stand up for herself. Without him gently, firmly urging her on, trying mightily to control his own anger, she didn't know if she would have pressed charges, much less been willing to go to court to tell her story yet one more time. Each time she recited it, it got worse for her, not better.

But the latter never turned out to be necessary. She was spared the courtroom ordeal. Jeff Downey confessed at the last minute and the case was settled out of court with a plea bargain. He was sent upstate and got ten years. Less with good behavior. He was paroled six months ago. Which meant he was out there somewhere. She tried very hard not to think about that.

She'd always suspected that her father had had something to do with Jeff's confession and his accepting the plea bargain, that somehow, Josef had managed to put pressure on the boy she'd once thought was the answer to her prayers instead of being the source of recurring nightmares. Her father had denied doing anything out of the ordinary when she asked.

But she knew her father, knew how he felt about all of them. How he felt about her being violated. There was nothing more important to Josef Pulaski than his wife and his daughters.

Although logically, she knew that not everyone had parents like hers, in her heart she always envisioned her parents whenever people mentioned their own. It was always sad to find out the opposite was true. Those were the times when she felt really lucky.

"It was," Jesse agreed. His father had been a stern man, but fair. They were just beginning to get along when Jason Steele was murdered. "But I got through it."

Interested, Tania asked, "What about your mom? How did she handle it?"

"She sold the store, bought a flower shop instead. Most people don't rob flower shops." He remembered how he begged her not to buy another store and how she'd tried to reassure him with statistics about flower shops. He still went there every day after school—to guard his mother until she closed up. "And she managed." He paused, wondering how the blond-haired doctor with the killer legs and the sweet smile had so effortlessly gotten so much information out of him. "Is this part of the treatment?"

"Sorry, my attending always says I get too close to my patients." Which wasn't strictly true, Tania added silently. She asked questions, but she didn't get close. Getting close involved vulnerability. She hadn't gotten close to anyone since the incident. Not even to the men she'd gone out with since then. She didn't know how.

He eyed her for a second, as if he was trying to make up his mind about something. "Do you?" he asked. "Get too close?"

She didn't answer him directly. She gave him a reply she felt worked in this case.

"I find patients trust you more if you take an interest in them. And I am interested in them," she assured him. "If I wasn't, I wouldn't be in this field." Smiling, she mentioned the first job she could think of that had to do with solitude. One she'd actually considered, except that solitude meant that she would be alone with her thoughts, and that she couldn't do. "I'd be a forest ranger."

"A forest ranger," he repeated, amused. "That would have been the medical world's loss."

Tania laughed softly. "Well, I see your encounter with the thief didn't knock the charm out of you." Pushing back the surgical tray, she stripped off the rubber gloves and deposited them into the trash bin. "We're done here," she announced, then took a prescription pad out of her lab coat pocket and hastily wrote something down.

"There might be pain," she warned him, tearing off the paper. "You can get this filled at your local pharmacy, or use the hospital's pharmacy." She gave him directions since he was probably unfamiliar with it. "It's down in the basement, to right of the elevator bank when you get off."

Jesse took the prescription she held out to him and glanced at it. His eyebrows drew together in consternation. He was looking at scribble. "You sure it says something?"

Tania grinned. Her mother, she-of-the-perfect-handwriting, used to get on her case all the time. "It does look like someone dipped a chicken in ink and had it walk across the paper, doesn't it? That was my first inkling that I was going to be a doctor. I have awful handwriting."

Jesse folded the paper and put it into his wallet. "Not awful…" he said with less than total conviction, letting his voice trail off.

Before she could say anything, someone behind her asked in a jovial voice, "So, how is the hero?"

They both looked over to the trauma room's entrance. The man whose diamonds he'd recovered stood in the doorway, beaming at him. There was a butterfly bandage on his cheek but other than that, he seemed none the worse for wear.

Tania pushed her stool back, then rose to her feet. "Good as new," she declared, then turned back to Jesse. "Now comes the really hard part." Her mouth quirked. "Filling out the insurance forms." She turned to lead the way out. "You can do that at the outpatient desk."

Isaac stepped into the room. He raised both hands, as if to beat the notion back. "No need. It's on me. I'll pay it," he told Jesse eagerly.

Jesse slid off the table, picking up his jacket. "That's all right," he told the older man. "My company has health insurance. They'll take care of it."

Isaac gave him a once-over, taking in the torn trouser leg and the stains. "Then a new suit," he declared with feeling. "I owe you a new suit."

For just a second, there was a mental tug of war. But in the end, pride prevented Jesse from taking the man up on his offer. The suit he had on had set him back a good five hundred dollars because he knew appearances were everything.

But he was his own man. He always had been. That meant he paid his own way and was indebted to no one.

"No," he assured the old man, "you really don't owe me anything."

This could go on all afternoon, Tania thought. She gently placed a hand to each man's arm and motioned them out of the room. "I'm afraid that you two need to settle this outside." She smiled brightly at Isaac. "We need the room."

Isaac began backing out immediately. "Of course, of course." He took both of her hands into his, his gratitude overflowing and genuine. "Thank you for all that you did."

Jesse debated slipping on his jacket, then decided to leave it slung over his arm. A dull ache started in his shoulder. He was going to feel like hell by tomorrow morning, he thought, remembering his days on the gridiron.

"What about you?" he asked the old man as they walked out of the room. "How's your face?"

Isaac touched the bandage, then dropped his hand. Even the slightest contact sent a wave of pain right through his teeth.

"If Myra, my wife, was alive today, she would say 'as ugly as ever.'" He shrugged philosophically. "When you are not a good-looking man, a blow to the face is not that big a tragedy." And then he smiled, nodding at his Good Samaritan. "Not like with you." He stood for a moment, cocking his head like wizened old owl, studying the doctor's handiwork. "Nice work. My brother Leon would approve. Leon is a tailor," he explained. And then his eyes lit up. "Of course. I'll send you to Leon." The thought pleased the jeweler greatly. "He will make you such a suit. And I will pay him."

How did he get the old man to understand that he didn't owe him anything? That successfully coming to the jeweler's rescue was enough for him. "No, really, I don't—"

But Jesse got no further in his protest. Isaac pursed his lips beneath his neatly trimmed moustache and beard. "Pride is a foolish thing, young man." He wagged his finger to make his point. "It kept the Emperor without any clothes." His voice lowered. "Please, it'll make me feel better."

Tania passed the two men on her way to get the chart for her next patient. "I'd give in if I were you," she advised Jesse. "It doesn't sound as if he's about to give up." And then she winked at the old man, as if they shared a secret. "Trust me," she told Jesse, thinking of her father, "I'm familiar with the type."

And with that, she hurried off to a curtained section just beyond the nurses' station.

Isaac watched her walk away. There was appreciation in the man's sky-blue eyes when he turned them back to Jesse. "Nice girl, that one." And then he asked innocently, "Are you married?"

"What? No." Was the man matchmaking? Trying to line up a customer for a ring? Well, he wasn't in the market for something like that right now. Maybe later, but not for a couple of years or so. "And not looking for anyone right now, either," Jesse emphasized.

His words beaded off Isaac's back like water off a duck.

"Sometimes we find when we don't look. And should you find," Isaac said, digging into his pocket, "you come to me." Producing a business card, he tucked it into Jesse's hand. "I will take good care of you. I'll match you up with the finest engagement ring you've ever seen." And then he added the final touch. "On the house."

Jesse nodded, pocketing the card, fairly certain that this was an empty promise the old man felt he had to make. Once there was a little distance from the events of today, Jesse was confident the man would feel completely differently. He had no intentions of holding a man to a promise made in the heat of the moment.

Besides, the last thing he needed right now was an engagement ring.

"And you, do you have a card?" Isaac asked him curiously, his bright blue eyes shifting to Jesse's pants' pocket.

Just by coincidence, he'd been given his first batch of cards yesterday afternoon. He hadn't had a chance to hand any out yet. "Yes."

Isaac waited for a moment. When nothing materialized, he coaxed, "May I have it? So that I can have your phone number," he explained. A gurney was being ushered by. Jesse and Isaac stepped to the side, out of the way. "Not to bother you, of course, but to see how you are doing and to find out when you are available for that suit."

Maybe saving this man's diamonds hadn't been such a good thing, after all, Jesse mused. Then again, maybe he was being a little paranoid. After all, the man was justifiably grateful. But after what he'd been through recently with Ellen, well, it had him still looking over his shoulder at times.

"Believe me, it's really not necessary."

Isaac fixed him with a long, serious look. "Neither was coming to my rescue, young man, but you did. Isaac Epstein does not forget a kindness. You are a very rare young man." So Jesse dug into his pocket and handed the man his card. "Jesse Steele," Isaac read, then glanced at what followed. "You are an architect?"

It had been a long road to that label. He still felt no small pride whenever he heard it applied to him. "Yes, I am."

"You know—" Isaac leaned his head in as if he was about to impart a dark secret "—my house could use expanding..."

Jesse couldn't help laughing. Isaac was harmless and well-meaning, if pushy. He put his arm across the older man's shoulders, leading him out of the area and to the outpatient station so they could both get on with their lives—especially him.

"I think we need to get out of everyone's way, Mr. Epstein." The police had indicated that he could come in later and give his statement, for which he was extremely grateful. "And I need to get to my office."

They weren't going to hold the meeting for him forever, he thought. He had a change of clothing at the firm, in case he had to take a sudden flight out on business. The suit might be wrinkled, but anything was better than what he was currently wearing.

"Let me make a call," Isaac offered. "My cousin's son, John, he owns a limousine service. You can arrive to your office in style."

"I can arrive on the bus," Jesse countered as he walked down the hallway with the older man.

Isaac released a sigh that was twice as large as he was. "I never thought I would meet anyone more stubborn than my Myra."

Jesse tried to keep a straight face as he said, "Life is full of surprises, Mr. Epstein."

"Isaac, please," the man corrected him as they turned a corner.

A little more than two hours later the flow of patients temporarily became a trickle. It was then that Shelly Fontaine, a full-figured nurse with lively eyes and a quick, infectious smile, came up to her, dangling a watch in the air in front of her.

"What would you like me to do with this, Dr. Ski?" The name was one Tania had suggested after Shelly's tongue had tripped her up several times while trying to pronounce her actual surname.

Glancing up from the computer where she was inputting last-minute notes, Tania hardly saw the object in question.

"Have Emilio take it down to Lost and Found where everything goes," she murmured. And then her mind did a double take. "Hold it," she called to Shelly who moved rather fast when she wanted to. "Let me see that again." She held her hand out for the watch. Upon closer examination, she recognized it. The timepiece was old-fashioned with a wind-up stem. And, if she wasn't mistaken, it had come off Jesse Steele's wrist. She had assumed he'd put it back on after she'd examined the scratch beneath the band. Obviously not.

But just to be on the sure side, she asked, "Where did you get this?"

"Trauma bay one." Shelly nodded back toward the room where, even now, another patient was being wheeled in on a gurney. It looked as if the flow was picking up again. "You were taking care of that hunk in there." Shelly's mouth widened in a huge, wistful grin. "I thought you might know where to find him. Assuming this is his and not some patient who was there before him."

"No, this is his," Tania said with certainty. "I recognize it."

It would be too much of a coincidence for there to be two watches like this worn by patients occupying the same room on the same day. Rather than give the watch back to the nurse, Tania slipped the watch into her pocket. Hitting several more keys, she saved what she'd input and rose from the desk.

"His address has to be on file," she said, thinking out loud. She knew for a fact that she'd seen it written on the information form the nurse had taken before she'd come in to treat the man. "I'll look it up and have someone mail it to him."

Shelly sighed soulfully as she followed her away from the desk. "I'd like to mail me to him."

"Shelly, you're married," Tania pointed out.

"I'm married, I'm not blind. I can look. And maybe lust," the older woman added mischievously. "It's not like Raymond doesn't look every woman over the age of eighteen up and down when he passes them."

Obviously not every marriage was made in heaven, Tania thought.

"Hey, you ready?" Kady called, coming around the corner like a runaway steamroller.

Tania made a show of looking at the watch on her wrist. "For lunch or dinner?" It was a blatant reference to the fact that her older sister was more than half an hour late.

"Sorry, it's been crazy today. I had to perform an emergency cardiac ablation. This man had an attack of atrial fibrillation that just wouldn't stop. I know I should have called, but there wasn't any time—"

"Save your apologies." Tania grabbed her purse from the drawer beneath the nurse's desk. "You lucked out. It's been hectic here all morning, too."

"Did it have anything to do with the camera crews outside?" Kady wanted to know.

She hadn't seen the light of day since she'd walked in yesterday. Armageddon could have swept the street of Manhattan and she wouldn't have known about it. "Camera crews?"

"Yeah, outside the E.R." Only extremely tight security, instituted right after the serial killings that had rocked the hospital last January, had kept the pushiest of the crew members out. "Something about a hero saving a dealer's diamonds. Security kept them out, but I heard that the media swarmed all over the guy when he finally left the hospital."

Tania shook her head. "Poor man probably never got to go to his meeting."

Kady stopped walking and looked at her sister, confused. "Meeting? What meeting?" And then the answer dawned on her. "Did you treat him?"

Stopping by the elevator, Tania pressed for the basement where the cafeteria was located. "I sewed up his scalp wound."

Kady sighed. "Some girls have all the luck," she teased. Tania looked at her and for one moment Kady could have bitten off her tongue. Because for one unguarded moment, Tania had allowed the pain to come through and register in her eyes.

But the next, Tania was flashing the wide smile she'd always been known for and nodding her head in agreement. "Yeah, we do. Your turn to buy lunch, by the way."

Kady was relieved that the moment had passed. "I distinctly remember that it was your turn."

"Maybe you should be marrying a neurosurgeon instead of a bodyguard. There's something going wrong with your memory."

The elevator arrived and the doors opened. Kady put her arm around Tania's shoulders and guided her in. "Not today, little sister, not today."

Chapter 3

She'd just wanted to make sure he was all right.

She'd been a safe distance away, trailing discreetly behind him—far enough away not to be noticed, close enough to see—when Jesse had stopped that thief.

Her breath had caught in her throat as she'd watched the two grapple on the ground. And it had taken everything she'd had not to run up to Jesse when she'd seen the blood trickling along the side of his head. She'd wanted to clean the wound with her handkerchief and make it better with her kisses.

In all probability, she *would* have run up to him to do just that, but the ambulance had arrived in the blink of an eye. When it had, rather than step forward she'd melted back in with the crowd. That was when she'd read the logo on the side of the vehicle. It had been dispensed from Patience Memorial Hospital.

She knew where that was.

Several months ago they'd treated her there when her wrists had had an unfortunate meeting with a shard of glass. The police had brought her there, summoned by her nosy superintendent who'd come about the overdue rent and had illegally let himself in when she hadn't answered the door. The police had wanted to label it a suicide attempt. She'd talked them out of it, saying it was just an accident. A glass had broken when she was washing dishes and she hadn't realized it until the jagged edges had scraped against both of her wrists and she'd felt faint.

They didn't look like they believed her, but she'd convinced them. She was good at convincing people when she set her mind to it.

Except for Jesse.

But then, Jesse was different. Special. He always had been. She'd known that from the moment she'd first seen him walk through the doors of the firm she worked for. Used to work for, she corrected herself. They'd fired her. Didn't matter. Nothing mattered. Except for Jesse. He was special.

Special. And hers.

He was so brave, so selfless. So willing to put everyone else first. That's why she loved him. Or at least that was one of the reasons. There were so many. She'd need a lifetime to count them. A lifetime that they would spend together.

Once she knew where the ambulance was going, she took off, availing herself of shortcuts in order to get there before the vehicle arrived. She succeeded, beating out the ambulance by a couple of minutes. Even using the siren, it had been slow going. The streets were clogged with lunchtime traffic and there was nowhere for the cars to pull over.

She'd counted on that, on the ambulance arriving at the rear E.R. entrance just as she had. She was in time to see Jesse being taken in.

Because there was so much activity in the immediate area, what with two other ambulances arriving on the heels of the first and the usual general commotion that occurred around an emergency room at midday, she managed to slip in without even being noticed.

She'd gotten very good at slipping in without being noticed.

Just like a little fly on the wall, she thought, her lips framing a smile that didn't quite move into her soul.

When the fluffy-looking blonde in the lab coat approached Jesse, she'd felt a sharp flare of temper, a surge of red-hot jealousy, but she banked it down. Her anger could be kept in abeyance as long as she thought that the woman was there to help Jesse. Jesse's well-being came first. Always. Besides, he didn't like shallow types like the blonde. He liked women like her.

He liked her.

Loved her, she silently corrected.

As the minutes ticked away, she finally managed to pass by the room where Jesse was being treated, peering in through the window. He wasn't looking in her direction, so he didn't see her. Which was good. But it was so hard to resist the temptation to rush in, to throw her arms around him and tell him that she would take care of him. That she was so proud of him for saving that old man's property but that he must never, never do that again. He could have been killed. What if that horrible man he'd brought down had had a gun?

She couldn't bring herself to think about it, it was just too awful.

She hated that man. Hated him for bruising Jesse's beautiful skin, for making Jesse hurt his head. If she could have, she would have made the thief pay for what he did. She would have stabbed him, then laughed as she watched the life dribble out of him. Someone like that didn't deserve anything better.

But those stupid policemen kept hanging around. They'd probably arrest her if she punished that man and gave him what he so richly deserved, what he had coming to him.

Jesse had almost seen her when he left the hospital, but she was too fast for him. She was certain that if he had seen her, he would have recognized her even though she wore a disguise.

The heart sees what the eyes don't.

And he loved her, she knew that. He was just a little confused, that's all.

He'd loved her once and you just don't stop loving someone. You don't.

She'd slipped out of the hospital close behind him when he'd left, but she'd managed to mix in with all the cameramen and reporters outside. She'd been tempted to shove one or two of the women. Women with their perfect hair and their pretty makeup, all trying to get close to Jesse. But she didn't. She'd kept her cool. Jesse would have been proud of her had he known.

He'd know soon.

Walking back to her apartment, she clenched and

unclenched the hands that were thrust deep in her pockets. She had to be patient. She'd make her move soon, but not yet.

Not yet.

It was oh so hard being patient. But it was a small price to pay for forever.

She was sure Jesse would agree.

Tania chewed on the inside of her lower lip, staring at the watch sitting on the desk in front of her. She'd almost forgotten about it until she'd shoved her hands into her pockets as she'd walked out of yet another trauma room and her fingers had come in contact with the leather band.

Jesse's watch.

In all the commotion this morning and his hurry to get to his meeting, had he just forgotten it? Or had he left it behind on purpose, left it behind so that he'd have an excuse to see her again?

Tania sighed. She had to stop being so paranoid. Sometimes an oversight was just an oversight, nothing more.

Even if Jesse *had* orchestrated this, the man had no way of knowing that a) she'd be the one to find the watch, which she actually wasn't, and b) that she'd opt to deliver his watch back to him in person. The most logical way to get this back to Jesse was just to have someone ship it out, the way she'd already mentioned to Shelly when the nurse had brought the watch to her.

But then, she wasn't the type to make someone do things for her that were not in some way directly related to hospital procedures. And even then, she had a tendency to try to do everything herself. Her sisters teased her and called her an overachiever. On occasion, Sasha had bandied about the word "controlling," trying, she knew, to make her come around and relax.

She supposed that "controlling" was actually more on target as far as assessing her behavior. She'd always been an overachiever, they all were in her family. But controlling, well, that was a later development. One designed to make her feel more secure.

If you controlled everything around you, or at least as much as possible, then you never had anything unexpected happening to you. You stayed safe. She had made a vow at seventeen never to be at the mercy of circumstances—and especially not at the mercy of any person.

She eyed the watch again, then made up her mind. Her endless shift was just about to finally come to an end. It would be no great hardship for her to drop this off on her way home—provided that the man didn't live in Connecticut, she mused.

Tania laughed softly to herself. If he did, this was definitely going into the mail. She was not about to go out of her way for any man, even if that man happen to be drop-dead gorgeous. That sort of thing no longer carried any weight with her.

Just the opposite was true.

Rising from the desk and dropping the watch back in her pocket, she went to outpatient registration to get Jesse Steele's home address.

He didn't live in Connecticut, or any of the other outlining states, either. As it turned out, when Sally Richmond "conveniently" turned away from the computer screen to let her look without actually saying she could,

Tania discovered that Jesse Steele lived right here in Manhattan, just the way she and her sisters did. Jotting the address down on an index card, she whispered, "Thank you" to Sally and slipped away from the outpatient registration area.

Hanging up her lab coat in her locker and resuming her civilian life, Tania took the crosstown bus to the address she'd written down. She'd taken care to write it in big block letters because she had just as much trouble reading her own handwriting as everyone else did. And given the choice of winding up in the wrong part of town or not, she'd choose "not."

It wasn't that much of a ride. Had she had more energy, she would have walked and probably gotten there faster, but by the end of her second shift, she was more or less drained. It had been a hell of a grueling sixteen hours.

So what are you doing playing messenger girl?

She had no answer for that.

After getting off the bus, Tania walked one block over until she reached the address on the card. She and her sisters had grown up in Queens, but they'd all made the trip into Manhattan, to take in the sights and wander the streets every chance they got. She knew the city like the back of her hand. Better.

While on the bus, she'd made up her mind to leave the watch with the doorman if there was one.

There wasn't.

The wide glass door leading into the modern highrise was unattended.

Doormen were swiftly going the way of the elevator operators of the last century. Into the mist.

As luck would have it, someone was just entering the building. Not wanting to ring bells at random, Tania slipped in behind the woman before the door closed again.

There was a bank of mailboxes along the far wall. Crossing to them, she scanned the names and apartments until she found "Jesse Steele, 10E." His was the only name listed. He lived alone.

Or maybe with someone who hadn't put up her name yet.

That made no difference to her, she insisted silently.

Tania pressed for the elevator. It must have been on the floor above because it arrived almost immediately.

She'd just leave his watch on his doorstep, she decided. Just before she'd left P-M, she'd taken an envelope with the hospital logo on it and placed the watch inside. Taking the envelope out of her purse, she sealed it as she rode up the elevator. There was no harm in leaving the watch on his doorstep. It'd be safe until he got home—provided he was out. The building was in the better part of town and it looked very respectable.

Stepping off the elevator, she began reading the numbers on the doors. The floor was tastefully done in subdued blues and grays, with paintings of flowers scattered through spring meadows hanging every few feet. It made for a pleasant, soothing atmosphere.

Apartment 10E was at the end of the hall.

Since she was just going to leave the watch on the floor directly in front of the door, Tania really couldn't explain what made her ring the doorbell at the last moment.

Even as she pressed the button, she turned away and started to retrace her steps to the elevator.

As it turned out, Jesse must have been on his way out,

because she'd only managed to take three steps before the door to his apartment swung open.

Jesse had trained himself to look through the peephole before opening the door. It wasn't his way, but better to be safe than sorry. Technically, he no longer had to be on his guard like this. The restraining order was in force and would continue to be for some time. And there hadn't been any incidents for a while now, not since he'd moved. For a while there, though, he'd found out firsthand exactly what a buck had to feel like during hunting season. And, granted there hadn't been any incident since the restraining order had been taken out, but he still wasn't a hundred percent at his ease. Someday, he hoped, he could reclaim his life and go back to being laid back, or at least not feel edgy every time he heard the doorbell ring.

But for now, he had to remain vigilant.

And surprised.

The woman's back was to him and she wasn't wearing a lab coat, but he recognized the soft sway of her hips immediately. It was part of what had caught his attention to begin with.

"Dr. Pulaski?"

Tania turned around, forcing a bemused expression to take over her features. She made a point of appearing nonchalant, so much so that no one except her family would have even remotely guessed at the tension she lived with every waking moment.

To the untrained eye, the smile was warm, perhaps even a little inviting. "Hi."

What was she doing here? Not that he minded, of course. This spared him the chore of coming up with a reason for going back to the hospital to try to see her again before he was scheduled to have his stitches rechecked.

"I thought house calls had gone the way of the dinosaur—or is there a problem with my insurance?" he joked.

She'd been on his mind, off and on, since he'd fought his way past the camera crew, shielding the jeweler while he was at it. The people he worked with were far more interested in having him retell the events of what had happened than they were in his contributions to the meeting he'd ultimately wound up missing. And then he'd had to stop at the precinct to give his statement. All the while, his thoughts kept straying to the woman who had tended to his wounds, vacillating between wondering if he'd ever see her again to *wanting* to see her again.

"No, no problem that I know of," she qualified. "But you did leave without your watch," she told him. She indicated the envelope on the floor.

"My watch." A look of astonishment slipped over his face as he looked at his wrist. Running behind all day, he'd chosen not to look at his watch, confirming just how late he was. If he had, he would have realized that it was missing.

And remembered where he'd last seen it.

Now *that* would have been a legitimate excuse to see her again.

"I didn't even know it was gone," he confessed, opening the envelope. "I'm so used to it being there, I thought it was. What do they call that, phantom something or other?"

"I think you're trying for 'phantom pain' and that only involves amputated limbs, not missing wristwatches." She didn't bother suppressing an amused smile.

He put the watch back on, then looked at it, relieved and satisfied all at the same time. "You have no idea how much this means to me."

"Obviously a lot." Which made her glad she'd gone out of her way to bring it back to him.

"It belonged to my father," he told her.

She'd already figured out that it was old. "That would explain the winding stem," Tania commented.

"My mother gave it to me when I graduated high school, said she knew he'd want me to have it." Not ordinarily an emotional person, he remembered fighting tears when he'd opened his gift and seen the watch. "It belonged to my grandfather before him."

"So passing it on is a family tradition."

The thought made her smile, not in amusement but with a feeling of empathy. Despite the fact that they had come to this country from their native Poland with hardly anything more than the clothes on their backs, her parents were very big on family tradition.

She needed to get going. She'd promised Kady to help her decide on wedding invitations. "Well, I'm glad I could reunite the two of you."

Tania paused for a moment longer. Everything told her she had to leave, but there was something about him, something warm and inviting that had her lingering just a second more.

To keep from looking like some kind of idiot who said one thing but did another, she asked, "By the way, how's your head?"

She looked even better without her lab coat. And probably excellent with less on than that. Jesse squelched the thought.

"It hurts," he admitted.

"That's what the prescription for the painkillers is for," she reminded him. Had he forgotten to get it filled?

But Jesse slowly shook his head, the way someone would if they were afraid their head would fall off. "I'd rather not take them if I can help it."

Oh, another one of those, she thought. "Macho, huh? I have a father like that. Do yourself a favor, take the pills." She second-guessed his reasons for doing without. "A few doses aren't going to make you slavishly dependent on them."

His best friend in high school had succumbed to addiction. And then just succumbed. Life was long and he intended to enjoy it. Unencumbered. But he had no desire to get into that now. So Jesse merely shrugged it off.

"I know, but it's really not that bad," he told her. Realizing that he was still standing in the doorway, he opened it a little wider and stepped back. "Can you come in for a minute?"

It was Tania's turn to shake her head. For all intents and purposes, he seemed nice. But no one knew where she'd gone and there was no way she was about to walk into his domain.

Come into my parlor, said the spider to the fly.

Jesse Steele didn't come across like a spider, but then, neither had Jeff. There was absolutely no way she was ever going to be anyone's fly again, anyone's victim. Everything was always going to be on her terms, or not at all.

"I can't," she answered. "I need to get home," she added. "I just thought you might miss your watch and I wanted to drop it off."

He seemed disappointed, but didn't push. "I would

like to pay you back for going out of your way," he told her. "Dinner?"

"Not tonight," she began.

He'd already assumed that. "Tomorrow?" he queried, then asked, "The day after?" when she didn't answer.

Despite her efforts to the contrary, she was amused. "If I say no, are you going to keep going?"

He nodded, crossing his arms before him. "Pretty much."

"What if I have a jealous husband?" she asked with a straight face. Did a little thing like marriage make a difference to him? Or was he accustomed to getting his way whenever he wanted something?

She saw him looking at her left hand, then raise his eyes again. "Do you?"

It was the perfect excuse, the perfect out. All she had to do was say yes and walk away. Something inside of her played devil's advocate and kept her from cloaking herself in the lie.

It was almost as if she was daring herself, seeing how far she would go. To see how far she would inch along the plank before it would bend beneath her weight, threatening to make her fall into the water. It was her usual modus operandi. She'd always scramble back to safety, but it seemed that each time she pushed herself a little harder, a little further.

Someday, she was going to hit that water.

No, she wasn't, she thought with confidence just before she answered his question.

"No, I don't."

"Good, then I'll just keep going." He thought a moment. "I think I was up to Thursday. Thursday night?" he asked.

She tried not to laugh. "I—"

Jesse just kept going. "Friday, then. Or Saturday. Saturday work for you?"

She gave up and laughed, shaking her head. "Okay, okay, dinner. Wednesday evening. You pick the place, I'll meet you there."

"I could pick you up," he offered.

"You could meet me there," she countered.

He looked at her for a long moment. "Are you sure there's no husband?"

"Just two nosy sisters."

He was an only child who had grown up longing for siblings. "You have two sisters?"

"Four, actually," she corrected. "Three older, one younger." And then she added with the same touch of pride that everyone in her family felt, especially her parents. "All doctors at Patience Memorial."

Now that was unusual, he thought, not to mention impressive. "Sounds like a really nice family."

Had he planned it, he couldn't have said anything better to her. Her family was everything to her. "It is. So, which restaurant?" He gave her the name of one and she nodded. "Expensive. Dinner there will probably cost more than that watch did when it was new."

"Some things," he told her, "you can't put a price on."

It was the sincerity in his voice that finally won her over. Part of Tania still felt that she might be making a mistake, since she really knew nothing about him except what he'd told her, but then, a man who comes to the aid of a stranger couldn't be all bad.

Right?

Chapter 4

Tania found herself looking at Kady as the latter threw open the door to the apartment she, Kady and Natalya shared.

"Well, it's about time. I was all set to fill out a missing person's report on you," Kady told her, one hand on her hip in a gesture that fairly shouted Mama. Apparently her older sister had flown to the door the second Kady'd heard her putting her key in the lock.

"Not me," Marja offered carelessly.

She came walking in from the kitchen after having foraged through her sisters' refrigerator. Her search had yielded a half-empty carton of chicken lo mein and she was well on her way to making it a completely empty carton.

Marja paused to render a wide, wistful smile. "I was all set to put my stuff in your room and move in."

"Antsy to get out from underneath Mama and Daddy's protective eye, are we?" Natalya laughed.

They'd all been there, all but smothered in genuine affection and concern. Not a one of them would have traded either of their parents in for any amount of riches. They all knew how very rare a couple Magda and Josef Pulaski were. Selfless, willing to work twenty hours a day if necessary to put them all through college and medical school.

Her father had said more than once that education was a blessing, which made it a family affair.

But right now, Marja was apparently focusing on the downside and she rolled her eyes in response to Natalya's teasing question.

"God, yes." The words were accompanied by a dramatic sigh. The drama she got from her mother. "I love them both to pieces, but they still think of me as a child," she wailed.

"No," Sasha corrected, keeping a straight face, "they think of you as the baby. The last little bird to fly out of the nest." She felt for her sister, but at the same time, she couldn't help teasing her. Lifetime habits were hard to break. "I'm not sure they're ready to acknowledge your flight plan, Marysia."

Marja preferred answering to her nickname, but she only allowed her family to use it. Didn't even mention it to anyone else. They had enough trouble with Marja. For the outsider, "Marysia" became nothing short of an unrewarding, gabled tongue-twister.

"Well, whether or not they acknowledge it, I'm out of there the second Natalya says 'I do' to Mike. I'm not even going to stick around for the reception," she said loftily, licking her fork to get the last of the lo mein, "just hitching the U-Haul to Sasha's car and bringing my stuff over."

Finished, she crossed back to the kitchen to throw the empty container out and toss the fork into the sink.

Natalya and Kady exchanged glances, shaking their heads. Marja might have graduated at the top of her graduating class, but she still had a bit of growing up to do.

Sasha grinned. As if leaving the house where she was born were that easy. One by one, they had moved out of the house in Queens, to be closer to the hospital where they all ultimately worked. Her parents had gone through the experience four times already. The fifth and last time was definitely not going to be a piece of cake, not if she knew Mama. Or Daddy, who was more versed than most about the kind of lowlife that was known to sometimes walk the streets of New York.

"Daddy will probably want to supervise," she told Marja. "You know how he is."

Marja sighed, planting herself beside Sasha on the love seat. "Yes, I do, God love 'im." It wasn't that she didn't have the utmost admiration and respect for her parents, and she did love them to death. She just wanted the opportunity to miss them once in a while. And to leave the house occasionally without verbally leaving a detailed itinerary in her wake. Whenever she tried, her father made it a point of telling her that he was asking because, just in case she went missing, they'd know where to start looking for her.

"Girls, they are going missing all the time," he told her with feeling. "You, we will not have missing. So, where is it you are going?"

Marja knew the dialogue by heart—and wanted to put

some distance between it and herself until such time as she could hear it without having it set her teeth on edge.

She glanced from one sister to another, looking for support. It wasn't as if this was something new, a phase their parents were going through. This was everyday life at the Pulaski residence.

"I just *really* need some time away from them. A vacation," she added because it sounded less harsh.

Natalya nodded, feigning sympathy. "Yeah, I know how it is. Hot meals, clean sheets, no rent to worry about, laundry done." She sighed loudly, shaking her head. "Must be hell."

"Oh, like you didn't leave the first chance you got," Marja reminded her.

"I had to. Sasha was lonely." She glanced toward her older sister. "Weren't you, Sasha?"

"I was too busy to be lonely," Sasha deadpanned.

"It's not that I'm not appreciative," Marja persisted. "It's just that I want them to stop looking at me as if I was their little girl." The others might not have thought so, but it really was no picnic, being the youngest.

"News flash." Perched on the arm of the love seat, Tania leaned over and pretended to knock on Marja's head. "You'll *always* be their little girl."

"We all will," Sasha interjected. "Even when we're in our nineties."

Marja shivered at the very thought. "Well, we need to fix that."

Sasha curved her hand protectively over her abdomen that was just beginning to swell. "Can't. It's a fact of life, Marysia. I'm already beginning to feel extremely protective and the baby's not even here yet."

Marja leaned over her older sister's stomach, cupping her hand to her mouth as she addressed the tiny swell. "Run, kid, run for your life. This is your aunt Marysia speaking. I know what I'm talking about."

"Idiot." Sasha laughed, thumping her youngest sister in the head affectionately.

If she didn't move this along, they'd never get to the reason they were all here. Kady looked at the last arrival. "I thought you said you were coming straight home to fall into bed." She'd all but had to twist Tania's arm to get her to agree to this get-together. It was called at the last minute because all five of them were very rarely off at the same time and she wanted everyone's input.

Tania's mouth curved in an enigmatic smile. She'd almost forgotten about that. "I was."

"Last-minute emergency?" Though their areas of expertise were all different—Sasha was an ob-gyn, Natalya, a pediatrician, Kady a cardiovascular surgeon, Tania was leaning toward spinal surgery while Marja thought about being an internist—they all knew how that was. One moment they could be walking out the door, the next they were being paged or button-holed to work on a patient who'd just been escorted in with flashing lights and sirens.

She wouldn't say that Jesse Steele constituted an emergency, but in some people's opinion—women people—he might be seen as a five-alarm fire. Still, she inclined her head and murmured, "Not exactly."

"Then what 'exactly'?" Natalya asked, exasperated.

Kady leaned forward on the sofa, her eyes narrowing as she carefully peered at Tania's face. "Wait, I know that face."

Tania drew back. "You should. I've had the room down the hall from you for—"

But Kady wasn't about to get distracted by an avalanche of rhetoric. She waved her hand for Tania to stop talking. "That's your I'm-going-out-with-a-new-guy face."

Intrigued, Natalya moved Kady out of the way and took her turn studying Tania's face. "You're right, it is." She looked properly impressed as she glanced back at Kady. "Boy, you're good."

Tania was on her feet. She wasn't in the mood to be teased. "You're all crazy. I expect this kind of thing from Mama, not you," she complained, slanting a glance to Kady and then Natalya.

As she began to turn away, Kady put herself directly in Tania's face. Of the five of them, Kady and Tania were the ones who looked most like one another. They all looked different. Their father was fond of saying that it was as if someone had given him a rose garden with five very different roses. Sasha had hair the color of midnight, Natalya was a vibrant redhead, while Marja's hair was golden-brown with red highlights shot through it. Natalya and Tania were both honey blondes.

"I'm afraid it's hereditary," Kady said with as straight a face as she could manage. "Something that's passed on from mother to daughter—"

"Like nagging?" Tania countered.

Natalya shook her head. "Uh-uh, don't let Mama hear you say that she nags. You will *never* hear the end of it."

"Which constitutes nagging," Tania declared. She spread her hands. "I rest my case."

"The hell with your case. Spill it," Natalya ordered.

"Who is it this time? You dumped poor Eddie less than three weeks ago." Eddie Richards was a fifth-year resident in pediatrics. "His body's not even cold."

"No," Tania agreed with a smile that Sasha had often called inscrutable, "but then, his body never was." And then she shrugged, as if tossing aside that part of her life. "But it was time to move on."

Like her parents and her sisters, Sasha worried about Tania, about the fact that Tania had had more boyfriends than the rest of them put together. There were times when Sasha felt that Tania acted more like a moving target than someone looking for a meaningful relationship, something that had, up to this point, never been part of her life. They all knew why and they gave Tania her space, but that didn't mean they weren't concerned.

If she wasn't careful, Sasha thought, Tania could very easily wind up on a self-destructive path. "You don't move on, you move around, like someone who—"

Tania shot Sasha a warning look. "Don't start, Sash. I'm too tired to go ten rounds with you, okay?" And then she looked at Kady. "I thought we were supposed to get together to hold your hand and help you make decisions about your wedding. I think we should do it quick before your groom comes to his senses and decides to head for the hills."

"Nobody's running anywhere," Sasha said in a quiet voice, purposely looking at Tania. "Running was never a solution." She let her words sink in before defusing any protest Tania might offer by saying, "I should know."

Sasha was referring to the way she was after her fiancé was killed right in front of her. Before Detective Tony Santini came into her life and they healed one another.

Well, things had worked out for Sasha, but that didn't mean that they worked out for everyone, Tania thought with a sigh. "If we're going to get serious, I'll drag out the tissues."

"Why isn't Mama here?" Natalya asked suddenly, realizing they were short one very vocal participant. "She likes to be in on these plans."

That would be her fault, Kady thought. "I just want to have a few things in place before Mama takes everything over."

"Mama doesn't always take over," Sasha said, defending the woman they all adored. Their mother meant well, she just was accustomed to doing things faster than waiting for someone else to do the task. She tended to be a little overzealous.

Tania laughed, shaking her head. "Right, and Napoleon ran a day-care center because he was so easygoing."

Just then, the doorbell rang. The five sisters all exchanged glances.

"Are you expecting anyone?" Tania asked Kady, but her question was meant for the others, as well.

"No," Kady answered.

"Not me," Marja chimed in, getting up again for another go at the refrigerator.

"You owe me dinner," Tania told her.

"Bill me," Marja said cheerfully, rummaging around again.

Natalya was on her way to answer the door. "Well, since none of us has X-ray vision, maybe someone should answer the door."

"Since you're on your feet anyway…." Tania let her voice trail off as she waved her older sister on.

"No respect for your elders," Natalya lamented, pulling the door opened.

"My thoughts exactly," Magda Pulaski agreed, walking in. As she passed her second child, Magda gently placed two fingers beneath Natalya's chin and pushed upward. "Close your mouth, dear. You are catching flies." She looked about at her other daughters. No one could tell if she was hurt, angry or just taking advantage of the moment and the element of surprise. "Why are you all leaving me out? Have I done something to offend you? Have I been a bad mother?" she asked. "Sasha, were you not happy with the wedding I helped you make?"

"It was a wonderful wedding, Mama." In truth, Sasha would have been satisfied exchanging her vows in whispers in the middle of the New York public library as long as her family was there and Tony was by her side.

"And you, you are not happy with the plans for your wedding?" she asked Natalya.

"Super plans, Mama," Natalya responded. It had taken about eight go-rounds, but now they were pretty super.

Kady slipped her arm around her mother's shoulder, stooping just a little because Magda was so short. "We're not leaving you out, Mama, we thought we'd do some of the preliminary work before taking up some of your valuable time and asking you for your opinion."

Magda frowned. She was versed to a greater or lesser degree in a dozen languages, but there were words in her adopted country that still eluded her. "I do not know what this 'preliminary' is, but if there is work to be done—" The look she gave Kady made her meaning clear. She meant to roll up her sleeves and pitch in from the very beginning.

Tania bit the side of her lower lip. A sign that she was uneasy. "We thought you'd be bored after planning two weddings."

"Bored?" Magda eyed her incredulously. "Bored is sitting at home, listening to your father tell the same stories over and over again." Sasha slipped behind her and handed her a glass of merlot, her mother's favorite variety of wine. Magda took it without skipping a beat, nodding at her oldest daughter. "I love that man, I really do. But he can be boring." She sighed. "So boring." And then she beamed. "Planning weddings for my girls is not boring, it is heaven."

Something wasn't adding up for Kady. Only the five of them knew that they were getting together. She'd gone out of her way to make sure the word didn't spread. "How did you find out we were having a meeting here this afternoon?"

Tania was on the receiving end of a beatific smile, as mysterious as it was amused. "I am a mother. Mothers always know when their children are up to something."

"And this all-seeing thing hits when?" Marja asked. "Right after the water breaks?"

Magda merely smiled. "I will let you find that out for yourself, Marysia," she promised. She sat on the sofa, taking a spot beside Kady. "All right, what have I missed?"

"Not a thing, apparently," Marja murmured under her breath.

Magda turned to look at her youngest, her line of vision straying toward Tania, as well. Rather than respond to what her youngest had commented, Magda's gentle hazel eyes widened.

"Oh, Tania, another one?" she asked. Surprise, dismay and sadness all mingled in her voice. "You are seeing someone new?" It wasn't really a question so much as a request for confirmation—or better yet, denial.

Stunned, Tania threw up her hands as she looked at her sisters for an answer. "How does she *do* that?" she cried helplessly.

The only answer she received was the concerned expression on her mother's thin and still remarkably unlined face.

The next moment, the previous moment was quickly swallowed up by chatter as catalogs were produced and questions and comments about the upcoming wedding flew back and forth across the room.

Magda Pulaski didn't believe in wasting time.

The next evening, when her shift was over, found Tania staring into the contents of her closet, looking over her clothing options. Her mind was elsewhere.

The ritual was always the same. An internal argument tantamount to an emotional tug-of-war would ensue every time she was about to go out with someone.

Every single time.

It didn't matter if it was the first date or the tenth— it had never gone beyond that number and rarely, if ever, even came close to it—she went through the same motions, the same wavering, undecided whether or not to go forward. If she canceled on the date, decided not to go through the hassles involved, then ultimately it meant that Jeff had won. Won because his presence, his memory, intimidated her.

Won because he made her afraid to live.

So, to "show" him, Tania would usually go ahead with her plans for the evening. Because she was so attractive and so seemingly outgoing, she wound up going out with a great many different men. Never becoming serious about any of them.

She'd laugh, perhaps even have a good time. But she was always split about things. So split internally that she never could fully experience anything that was happening. If she went to bed with a man, if her desire to negate Jeff's hold on her took her that route, it was only her body that was there. Emotionally, she always slipped away, too afraid of what the consequences of her actions might entail.

And her mental game of Ping-Pong always began here, in the bedroom, as she pondered the sanity of what she was undertaking while she moved hangers about in her closet, trying to pick out something to wear.

Just as she took out a dark blue sheath, she cursed under her breath.

No, damn it, she wasn't going to keep doing this. Jesse Steele was a nice guy, gave off nice-guy vibes, and it was just dinner, anyway. The man didn't even know where she lived and as long as she went to a crowded place, she'd be fine. They'd meet, eat, talk and then, for tonight, go their separate ways.

And then she would think about her options.

Nothing to worry about, she told herself sternly as she slid the zipper up the back of the sheath.

She didn't set out to like him.

Wasn't prepared to like him.

Didn't *want* to like him.

Liking someone only complicated things. You didn't have to like the person you were physically attracted to. Liking them got in the way of the sex and, when she came right down to it, that was as far as she ever planned things. To cap off the evening with sex. Sex that would—maybe this time—somehow disintegrate the memory of that other time. That time that had smashed her soul into tiny pieces.

But all that would come—if it came at all—later. She never, ever allowed herself to be coaxed into bed on the first date. She might be lost, but she wasn't easy. And things were done according to her plans, not anyone else's. She made the terms, she called the shots. She only allowed the man to think he was the aggressor. He wasn't. She was. And as the aggressor, she had the right to end it whenever she wished.

Still, Jesse made her laugh. More, he made her smile. Not just one of those fleeting smiles where the corners of her mouth quirked, but one of those deep, penetrating smiles that went clear down to the bone and made you glad to be alive.

In her case, it made her glad that she had decided to meet him for dinner instead of bowing out at the last minute, using her old standby excuse: I'm on call—and they called.

Half an hour into dinner, Tania caught herself actually thinking about shutting off her cell phone and wishing that she could. As far as she could remember, it was the first time that had happened.

"I read about you in the paper," she said as the waiter cleared away the few crumbs that were all that was left of a sinfully delicious appetizer.

Jesse winced at the mention of the coverage. "Please, the less said about that, the better."

His response aroused her curiosity. In her experience, most people tried to get into the limelight, not avoid it.

"Why?" She nodded a silent thanks to the waiter who now began to serve the main course. "I thought everyone liked getting their fifteen minutes of fame."

"Not me," Jesse said with feeling. The less attention he had drawn to him, the better. He'd already been the recipient of enough attention to last him a lifetime. More. "I'm perfectly satisfied to donate my fifteen minutes to someone else. As far as I'm concerned, they can have thirty."

Despite her best efforts not to, Tania found herself intrigued. Jesse looked as if he really meant what he said.

Chapter 5

Tania waited until the waiter retreated again before asking her question. "Are you just shy, or is it that you're harboring the soul of a hermit?"

"Neither." He turned his attention to the main course, discovering that he was pretty hungry. "I'd just rather not have the attention."

The signs were posted, she mused. This was where she was supposed to back off, to artfully change the subject to something light. Knowing things about other people eroded the barriers, theirs and hers.

But he'd made her curious. And besides, for the time being she had no desire to lapse into inane statements that fell in the category of "How 'bout those Yankees?"

So, even as she picked up her knife and fork, she fixed Jesse with her most penetrating, interested gaze and prodded a little.

"But why?" she asked him. "There has to be a reason why—" She added what she thought of as the clincher, "And you might want to get it off your chest."

No doubt she was thinking about confession being good for the soul. "It's nothing like that."

"Like what?" she asked innocently, silently urging him on.

To confess, he had to have done something wrong, and he hadn't, Jesse thought. Except pay attention to the wrong woman. It had made him gun-shy for a while. Until yesterday.

She was waiting, so he elaborated. "I'm not someone who jumped bail in another state, or a delinquent dad who's fallen so far behind in his child support payments that there's a warrant out for his arrest."

"Good to know." She didn't bother to add that he didn't seem like the type. She wasn't all that great a judge of character. Tania took a sip of her Long Island Iced Tea and then placed it back on the table. "You're also not shy because shy people don't spring into action. They hope someone else will do the springing so their conscience won't haunt them." Tania paused, waiting. But Jesse didn't take the bait.

She leaned in a little closer, creating a small, private world for the two of them. "Now you have me really curious. C'mon, get it off your chest. They say it's good to face your fears." She parroted what the therapist had said to her during her first—and only—session. The therapist was a friend of Natalya's and had a very gentle, soothing manner. But gentle, soothing manner or not, she just didn't have the desire to bare her soul to a stranger.

But Jesse didn't need to know that.

"True," he agreed. "But only if voicing them leads to conquering them. In my case, I could stand on a rooftop and conduct a thirty-minute monologue, it still wouldn't change the situation." He appeared rather complacent about the matter when he said, "I've already done everything that I could."

She couldn't make the pieces fit, couldn't second-guess what he was referring to.

"Okay, you're not leaving here until you spill your insides to me, Jesse Steele. I was just teasing before, but if there's one thing I can't stand," she told him honestly, "it's not knowing the outcome of something." She'd been like that as far back as she could remember. "That's why I finish every mystery I start reading, watch every horrible movie to its conclusion. I need to know things, even things of no interest, and I thrive on answers. You now have one of those in your possession." Her eyes teased him. "So give."

He laughed, not quite knowing if she was serious or not. "You're really making more out of it than it deserves."

"I'm not," Tania countered as bits of her salmon fillet continued to disappear from her plate, making their way into her mouth, "you are." She paused to level her gaze at him, issuing a royal decree. "So talk."

He was within his rights to tell her it was none of her business, because it wasn't. But he didn't want to say something like that to her. *Didn't* want to shut her out. So he took a long sip of his drink and began. "I made the mistake of dating a woman who worked for the same firm that I did."

The information was vaguely disturbing. There was no reason why it should be. After all, someone who looked like Steele wasn't destined to live life as a monk. And yet it bothered her, which made no sense to her.

Of course the man dated women before he asked you out. What did you expect? That he lived in a monastery before he was brought in strapped to that gurney? Monks just do not *have muscles like that.*

She deliberately kept her thoughts from registering on her face. Tania raised her glass to her lips before she nonchalantly asked, "A fellow architect?"

Jesse shook his head. "She is—was," he corrected himself, the very action giving him discomfort because despite everything, he did feel bad that she'd lost her job, "an administrative assistant."

Tania picked up on the one telling, all-important word. "'Was'?"

Jesse nodded. His appetite was slipping away. He forced himself to eat a little more. He wasn't the type to take home leftovers wrapped in aluminum that had taken on the shape of a swan. "The company let her go after certain behavior came to light."

He didn't look comfortable, Tania thought. Was that because he retained his position while the woman he was talking about had lost hers? Empathy engulfed her, coming out of nowhere.

She tried to lighten the moment. "They didn't approve of her making love with you in the supply closet?"

That was the ironic part, he'd never made love to Ellen at all. She'd spun her fantasies out of air and imagination, nothing more. "That wasn't the behavior they disapproved of."

Tania's eyes widened. "So she did make love in the supply closet with you. I'd thought it was understood that quick trysts in small, windowless enclosures were the sole domain of hospitals."

Not that she ever had done that, but she'd accidentally walked in on one of the nurses in more than a simple amorous clinch with an attending. Not hers, thank God, because that might have been the end of her career. Attendings didn't like being laughed at and she still wasn't able to look at the man without picturing him with his scrubs and his underwear around his ankles.

It would have been difficult taking orders from a man like that.

"No closets," he assured her. The topic, because it considered him, made Jesse uncomfortable. But there was no getting away from it now. He'd started it, he had to finish it. "Just a difference of opinion."

She wasn't sure she followed this. Tania looked at him quizzically. How did a difference of opinion lead to an employee being fired?

"About?"

He studied the last few drops in his glass. Amber, they caught the light and shimmered beneath it. "Whether or not there was a relationship between us. She thought there was one, I didn't."

"I take it she didn't like your version of things."

The laugh that escaped his lips had no humor in it. "Not in the least."

Well, now he had her hooked. "So what happened?" She wanted to know. "Did you find a rabbit in one of your pots?"

He counted himself lucky that it hadn't gone that route. But for a while there, he'd held his breath. "No, but I would come home to find her cooking dinner for me." It happened twice before he lost his patience and put an end to it.

Tania stared at him. "You gave her the key to your apartment?"

There had to have been some sort of relationship for that to have happened, she thought. Maybe he wasn't as innocent of blame as he seemed. Maybe he had led the woman on.

But his next answer negated that line of thinking. "No. Apparently she picked the lock."

"Resourceful."

Jesse frowned. "That makes her sound like a Girl Scout. Believe me, she wasn't." She was mentally damaged. Incapable of taking no for an answer. He sincerely hoped that she was getting the treatment she so badly needed.

His response begged for a question. "What was she?"

"As near as I can figure, a sociopath." There was no other label he could apply. Other than crazy. "I tried to make her understand that it just wouldn't work out between us, but it was like my words were just bouncing off her head and disappearing into the atmosphere. She acted as if everything was just fine. As if she belonged in my apartment. It took me forever to make her leave. The second time I found her there, she refused to go, said we belonged together for all eternity.

"When I tried to physically put her outside my apartment, she started screaming at me, pinching, kicking, biting. The neighbors called the police—" his mouth curved in an ironic smile "—who promptly proceeded to arrest me for abusing her. Ellen cheered them on. But when one of the policemen started to put handcuffs on me, she suddenly had an about-face and flew into a rage. She started pummeling the guy with her fists." His mouth curved a little more. "That was when they realized that maybe I wasn't the one at fault here."

"You think?"

Tania's sarcastic remark momentarily hung in the air between them. She felt as if she'd just crossed over a bridge and while she wasn't exactly close to Jesse, she was at least a little closer than she had been a moment ago. They'd both endured things at the hands of another that they shouldn't have.

Although the damage that she'd sustained as opposed to him were worlds apart, at least Jesse understood what it meant to be at the mercy of someone else.

"So then what happened?" she asked.

"They arrested her for assaulting an officer. I had no trouble taking out a restraining order against her. I don't know how—" because this was something he hadn't shared "—but someone at the firm got wind of the restraining order and what had caused me to take one out in the first place. Ellen was summarily dismissed before the end of the workday."

He'd felt genuinely bad about that. Ellen had told him she hadn't had much in the way of savings. Because he felt responsible, he'd been tempted to send her money to help tide her over. But when he mentioned it in a conversation with one of the senior partners, Alfred Bryce, the man immediately read him the riot act, warning him that Ellen would only misconstrue the gesture, thinking he'd committed to her, after all.

In his heart, Jesse knew that Bryce was right, but his conscience still bothered him.

"Ellen," Tania echoed, plucking the woman's name out of the array of information.

He nodded. He hadn't said her name out loud for six months now. That was how long he hadn't seen her. It was beginning to look as if he was finally home free, that Ellen seemed to have moved on. "That was her name. Ellen Sederholm."

The name made her envision someone petite and mousy, but that was probably unfair, Tania thought. "And where is 'Ellen Sederholm' these days?"

He'd heard via the grapevine that she'd moved, but he wasn't about to attempt to find out if she had. He could only hope that it was out of state.

"Not within five hundred feet of me is all I know or care about," he told her.

And then it all suddenly came together for her. "And that's why you didn't want your face on the five o'clock news—because you're afraid that it might set Ellen off again."

The way she said it, it didn't sound like a question but an assumption. He answered it anyway, even though it sounded a little egotistical.

"Something like that." Jesse's lips twisted into a small smile. "My mother taught me not to take foolish risks."

Obviously the man only reflected on that when it served his purposes. "And your tackling a fleeing, armed robber was, what, a smart risk?" She laughed, then added, in case he was about to claim that it hadn't really been that risky, "I saw the video someone got of you in action on their cell phone." There was no such thing as privacy left in the world, she thought. Someone was always filming you, invading your life in hopes of being able to sell what they captured to the news media and the highest bidder. "Looked pretty risky to me."

At the time he hadn't paused to weigh his options, he'd just reacted. Still, he shrugged. "Calculated risks are okay."

Tania just wasn't buying it. Mr. Epstein had been right. Jesse was a hero, the kind her father had always approved of. "And you had time for these calculations—when?"

She had him there, Jesse thought. "Are you sure you're a doctor and not a lawyer?"

Tania pressed her lips together, suppressing a laugh. He had no idea how funny his suggestion was. Her father would have gone into anaphylactic shock if she'd told him that she wanted to become a lawyer.

"I'm sure. My father would have never let me become a lawyer," she said with a fond laugh. She could just hear her father's voice, enumerating the many faults of lawyers. "Depending on the time of day you ask him, he thinks they're just a little above or a little below snakes on the food chain."

"Sounds like a man who has opinions," Jesse commented diplomatically as the waiter returned to discreetly refill his glass. "You take after him?" It was a question he already felt he knew the answer to.

"To an extent." Tania played with the stem of her own glass. The waiter raised one eyebrow in a silent query, but she shook her head. One was her limit. Never again was she going to relinquish her control to a hazy world just because she liked the taste of a particular drink. "Not that he would admit it. He thinks I'm stubborn and he's just being steadfast."

In truth, she and her father had had few arguments. Josef liked to indulge his girls. Mama, on the other hand, had been known to lock horns with everyone but Sasha. Sasha was too easygoing to be drawn into an argument.

Amused, Jesse asked, "And what is it that you're stubborn about?"

"Not always taking his advice."

Her father had wanted her to all but become a nun after the incident. He hadn't actually said so in so many words, but every time she went out, his face became a mass of concern. And then there was always an endless barrage of questions.

Granted, he was worried about her, and she was, too. But determination trumped worry and she was determined not to let Jeff's actions brand her.

At least, not any more than they already had.

She refused to become a hermit. But then, on every outing, fear always turned up somewhere within the course of the evening and shut her down. More than anything, she wanted to break the cycle. She wanted to be whole again.

"Tell me more about your father," Jesse coaxed.

She wondered if he was just making conversation or if he was hungry to picture a father, any father, because his own had been taken from him at a young age.

So she gave him details. "He was born in Poland. Warsaw," she added. "That's where he met my mother. And where he married her. They decided to come to this country when she became pregnant with Sasha. They both wanted their children to have the opportunities they hadn't had.

"They settled in Queens and Dad became a cop. That was where my sisters and I grew up. My parents still live in the first house they ever owned."

It was hard to miss the fondness in her voice when

she spoke about her parents, Jesse thought. It was clear that she loved her family.

"Marja, my younger sister, still hasn't flown the coop. But it'll probably happen anyday now."

"And your sisters are all doctors," he marveled, thinking that was an incredible feat.

Tania nodded. "Every last one."

"Your parents must be exceptionally well-off."

Tania laughed. "Not hardly. At least, not in the way you mean. As far as money goes, they both worked their fingers to the bone, putting us through school. And it was understood that the second each of us graduated, we were to help the next in line."

Finished, he moved back his plate. "That's an interesting take on the domino theory."

"My parents are interesting people," she responded. Tania paused to take a sip from her water glass to clear her palate.

Jesse wondered what it was like, being part of such a seemingly harmonious unit. What it felt like to have people to count on, people to turn to. "I'd like to meet them sometime."

Tania studied him for a moment. That had more than just a transient sound to it. But then, men said all sorts of things while they were orchestrating scenarios that hopefully guaranteed that they'd be in someone else's bed by evening's end.

She inclined her head. "Maybe you will—sometime," she qualified. She glanced at her plate and realized that she'd finished eating. "My God, I had no idea I was that hungry."

"You certainly did justice to it." He liked seeing a

woman who wasn't afraid to eat, who didn't feel compelled to pick at her food as if she were dissecting something toxic for a science project. "Would you like some dessert?"

She had a sweet tooth that demanded tribute whenever it could, so she nodded. "There's still a little room just under my rib cage," she decided. "The perfect space for ice cream."

"Ice cream it is," he promised. Jesse had only to raise his hand.

The next moment the waiter was hovering over their table again, ready to bring in dessert.

After dessert was savored and he had paid the check, they left the restaurant. When he began to hail a cab, she stopped him.

"It's such a nice night, let's just walk. It's not far," she reminded him.

"All right."

In a disarming gesture, she slipped her arm through his. "I like the city at night. It's subdued, elegant. The pulse isn't quite so frantic and people don't seem to be in as much of a hurry at night as they do in the daytime."

There was a reason for that. "That's because everyone only has thirty-eight minutes for lunch," he pointed out. "And a list of errands to run at least the length of their arm."

She laughed. "You have a point."

The warmth that seeped into her via the contact was subtle. It took a moment before she was even aware of it. She released his arm and then promptly felt awkward. Not that she'd taken his arm in such a familiar way but that she'd let it go in the next heartbeat.

If he noticed anything strange, Jesse gave no indication.

"I don't live far from here," she told him, forcing a cheerful note into her voice.

"I'm not afraid of walking," he assured her. "Sometimes the only exercise I get is walking."

She turned her head to look at him. "And other times?"

It was a loaded, leaded question. She waited to hear his response.

"And other times I get it from the gym. One of those thirty-day, free-trial deals. If I'm not satisfied with the results by then, I can get my money back."

Her eyes swept over him and she smiled. She'd seen him without his shirt on and could honestly say that he had a body other men would kill for. "I don't think you'll be getting your money back anytime soon."

He grinned. "Why, thank you."

She could feel the effects of his smile going straight through her gut. "Wasn't a compliment, just an observation," she pointed out.

Her building was just up ahead. How had they gotten here so soon? It was as if the minutes had just melted into one another, melting away faster than snowflakes landing on a radiator.

Taking a long breath, she stopped walking right by the building's doorway. "Well, we're here."

"Not yet," he contradicted. "We're not officially 'here' until I bring you to your door."

Where was this panic coming from? It had been going so well, too. But there it was, with sharp, pointy little cleats, making holes in her. She tried not to sound as if she was nervous. "That's not necessary."

His smile was reassuring. Some of the nervous flutter left her stomach.

"That all depends on which side of the testosterone you're on." Holding the door open for her, he followed her inside. The elevator was to the right and it was waiting for them. He pressed the button and the doors opened. "See, it's an omen. I was supposed to take you to your floor."

She made no reply. Instead she pressed the button for the fifth floor. When he glanced at her, there was a new expression in her eyes. Wariness? Why? He did what he could to make her comfortable.

"Don't worry, I won't ask to come in," he assured her softly.

"I wasn't worried," she said a bit too quickly. The doors opened and they got out. Shoulders slightly stiff, she led the way to her apartment.

It was a lie, Jesse thought. A concerned look had crossed her face. She seemed slightly distracted. Had someone forced himself on her? Pushed his way in at the end of a date and that made her leery of everyone who came in the guy's wake?

He wanted to ask, but knew that would only make her more tense.

"Good to know," he murmured as they stopped before a door he assumed was hers.

There was that smile again, she thought, watching it unfurl on his lips.

Feeling it unfurl within her, as well.

Chapter 6

One moment his smile was affecting her insides, turning them upside down. The next moment it touched her on the outside as Jesse brought his mouth down on hers.

Tania was conscious of everything within the immediate vicinity. Conscious of the roots of her hair all the way down to the tips of her toes, which were curling within her shoes. Warmth spread out from their point of contact to all parts of her, threatening an immediate meltdown. She felt his hands as, still kissing her, he gently framed her face.

Felt her own heart slip into double-time as the kiss deepened.

She struggled not to be swept away.

Ordinarily she was the one who set the pace, she was the one who knew when a kiss was coming, or when anything physical was going to transpire, because she initiated it. She was the one who called the shots. Always. But this time, she had barely gotten to the starting point before the gun was fired and the race had begun. She wasn't ready.

Deeply ingrained survival instincts pleaded for her to pull away, to stop this until it could transpire on her terms. But something else, something even stronger, something lost and needy, whispered, "Continue."

She didn't like the way she felt.

She loved the way she felt.

Her head spinning, she was both dizzy and exhilarated. The upshot being that she was hopelessly confused. So confused that rather than follow her instincts, instincts that had kept her safe for more than ten years now, Tania wove her arms around Jesse's neck. And continued.

She told herself she could handle this as she sank further into a kiss that offered no escape hatch, no way out, only a path further down into a fiery, all-consuming furnace.

Her lips moved over his, taking him with her into the inferno. If she was going to be incinerated right here on her own doorstep, she damn well intended to leave an impression on him.

Jesse couldn't catch his breath.

He was right. There was chemistry here. Enough chemistry to blow up an entire building if he wasn't careful. She numbed his mind and made him fervently wish he hadn't told her that he wouldn't ask to come into her apartment. Because he wanted to come inside her apartment, wanted to make love with her slowly, with feeling. Wanted to have his hands slip along a body he knew in his gut was soft and firm and inviting.

Desires collided with reason. Something told him that he needed to go slowly with this woman who could set him on fire simply with the sweet taste of her mouth. Not because Ellen had spooked him when it came to women, but because this lady doctor seemed to want to take it one measured step at a time.

She would be worth the wait.

The ringing noise intruded, cramming its way into his consciousness until he realized what it was. Taking a deep breath, Jesse reluctantly moved his head back and looked at her.

"You're ringing," he said, his mouth still so close that, as he smiled, she could almost feel the movement of his lips. "I'd take it as a compliment, except that I think it's your cell phone."

Her brain felt as scrambled as a hot pan filled with stir-fried ingredients. Dazed, she tried desperately to focus, to understand what he was saying. The ringing abruptly ceased.

"My phone?" Tania murmured, looking up at him. The trap she'd tried to set for Jesse had snapped shut around her instead. She wanted to go on kissing him, wanted to continue basking in the sensations he created for her.

And then Tania's brain finally engaged. "Oh, my phone."

Taking another long breath, Tania fumbled at her waist, searching for the cell phone she kept clipped there. Just as her fingers closed over it, about to remove the now silent phone so she could see who'd called, the door to her apartment opened.

The movement had Jesse looking in that direction. A redhead with green eyes stood in the doorway, the doorjamb framing her. If she was surprised, she hid it rather well. Amusement entered her eyes and when she smiled, her mouth moved in exactly the same way that Tania's did.

Her voice was almost melodic. "Tania, you brought home takeout."

And she took a closer look at him. Jesse knew recognition when he saw it. It wasn't his most comfortable moment, but then, it was something he told himself he was going to have to put up with for a while longer, until some other New Yorker did something print-worthy and took his place.

"You look very familiar," the redhead said. "Do I know you?"

Tania took the opportunity to pull herself together. When Jesse didn't answer immediately, she glanced at him. He seemed a little uncomfortable, as if he might think it presumptuous to say that Natalya recognized him from the newspaper or from a sound byte that had aired on TV.

He *was* shy, Tania thought. Somehow, that made her feel better, although for the life of her, she couldn't have explained why. "This is Jesse Steele, Natalya—" Tania got no further.

Her green eyes widened with admiration and pleasure. "The guy who tackled the jewelry store thief, right? My sister sewed you up. You must like her work." And then, before he could comment, Natalya grew serious for a second. She glanced over her shoulder into the apartment. Even as she did so, there was a murmur of voices. "Um, Tania, if you'd like him to come in, I can move everyone into my room."

Tania's eyebrows drew together. "Everyone?" she echoed. "Who's everyone?"

"That's all right," Jesse cut in. "I've got to be going. I was just saying good-night."

Natalya's amusement returned in spades. Her eyes washed over him appreciatively. "Yes, I noticed." She flashed Tania a smile. "It's up to you. I can—"

Tania knew better than to let her sister talk. There was nothing any of her sisters liked more than to playfully embarrass one another and this was perfect fodder for Natalya.

"He was just leaving," Tania said firmly, even though inside she caught herself wishing that he wasn't. That it was her sister and whoever comprised "everyone" who were leaving.

"A pity," Natalya said, giving Jesse one last once-over. "Well, it was nice meeting you, Jesse." She put her hand out to shake his. Her eyes darted from Tania back to him. "Don't be a stranger, now. There isn't always a three-ring circus taking place in the living room," she promised.

As if to negate her words, two more young women had come up behind Tania's sister. They both had Tania's eyes if not her coloring, Jesse noted.

He inclined his head toward Tania and said, "I'll call you," before backing away. The next moment he'd turned on his heel, intent on going back to the elevator.

Kady watched the man disappear while Marja craned her neck to get a better view.

"Nice," Kady commented wickedly, then glanced at Tania. "Who was that?"

"Nobody," Tania said before Natalya had a chance to tell them.

"'Nobody' has a really nice walk-away," Marja interjected. She turned around to look at Tania. "If you don't want him, I don't mind taking some of your castoffs…" Her voice trailed off with a hopeful note.

"He's not a castoff," Tania informed her.

Marja pretended to look disappointed. "Then you're keeping him?"

Tania closed her eyes, searching for patience. "He's not mine to keep or give," she insisted.

"Really?" Natalya looked completely unconvinced. "From where I was standing, you two looked pretty hermetically sealed."

Marja waved her hand at the so-called evidence. "This is Tania you're talking about, have lips, will travel. She's an equal opportunity kisser. Her hobby is breaking hearts, remember?"

Tania ignored her younger sister and changed the subject. She directed her question to Natalya. "So what's this about a three-ring circus in the living room? What's up?"

Natalya slipped her arm around Tania's shoulders and gave her a small squeeze, a show of unity in case Tania felt put upon.

"We're holding an impromptu meeting." And then Natalya inclined her head so that neither Marja nor Kady, walking ahead of them, could hear. "Go easy on this one, Tania. He looks like a keeper." Tania shot her a warning look. She wasn't in the mood to be teased. "Someone's, if not yours," Natalya added.

Tania merely shrugged at the unsolicited advice. Her sisters all knew that she was not in the market to do anything beyond being diverted.

"If you say so," she said dismissively, then looked around the living room. All four of her sisters, Sasha's husband and Natalya's fiancé, as well as Kady's, were there. This was apparently big, whatever it was. Had something happened to one of her parents? Ever since the incident, Tania did her best to present a happy face to her family, but her thoughts always veered to the dark side. "What is going on?" She wanted to know.

The first thing out of Natalya's mouth set her at ease. "We're brainstorming," her sister told her.

A sense of relief swept over Tania. Nat wouldn't have said that if something was really wrong. Whatever was going on, it wasn't life-threatening.

Her mouth curved as she glanced at the three men. "And, look, you brought in extra brains."

Tony Santini, perched on the arm of the sofa where his wife sat, held up his hands in silent disclaimer. "I'm just the driver, nothing more."

"Here for moral support," Mike DiPalma, Natalya's fiancé, chimed in.

"Same here," Byron Kennedy, Kady's fiancé, told her.

"And why is there a need for moral support?" Tania wanted to know, looking from one sister to another. "What is it that you're all brainstorming about?"

Since it was her problem, Sasha spoke up. "Mama's going a little overboard about this baby. Ever since she found out I was pregnant, she's been hovering and trying to get me to cut back my office hours." Sasha sighed. "Cut back my life, really. I think she's about to surround me with bubble wrap and I'm not even showing yet." The irony of the situation made her laugh. "You'd think that I wasn't an ob-gyn." Tony took her hand in his in a silent show of support. "There's nothing about giving birth that I don't know."

"Except how to handle Mama," Kady interjected with a sympathetic grin.

Sasha sighed and nodded her head. "Except how to handle Mama."

"Seems to me that Daddy should be in on this, don't you think?" Tania suggested, looking from Sasha to Natalya. "After all, he's the one who's survived with her all these years. That should give him a little insight into the matter."

Natalya looked at her as if she should know better. "Daddy's insight can be summed up by two little words. 'Yes, Magda.' He dotes on Mama and he's learned to placate her."

Sasha shook her head. "You'd think that having two weddings to help plan would be more than enough to keep Mama busy."

Tania laughed. Their mother was nothing if not a whirlwind. "You know Mama. Multitasking should have been called 'Magda-tasking' in her honor since she practically invented it."

As Kady began to put in her own two cents, Tania's cell phone went off again. The sound reminded her of the call she'd ignored earlier on her doorstep. She angled her cell phone's LCD screen to see who was calling her even as her sisters checked to see if it was their phones that were ringing.

"Mine," Tania declared with a note of resignation. "It's the hospital." So much for spending the rest of the evening at home. Taking the phone off the clip, she held off opening it for a second. "My advice is to get Mama entrenched in the idea that she's been toying with off and on for the last five years—her own catering business." She looked at Sasha. "That *plus* the two weddings should keep even Mama too busy to make you crazy."

Mama seemed to be tireless and to never need any sleep. Sasha had her doubts that even if they could convince her to finally turn her dream into a reality, that Mama would back off—even a little.

"If only," Sasha sighed.

As Tania turned away, placing the cell phone to her ear, Natalya took up the suggestion. "You know, Tania just might have something there. Mama loves to cook and she's really good at it." Her tone indicated that they had nothing to lose by championing the idea and bringing it to their mother's attention as a unit. "Hey, it's worth a shot."

Tania moved away from the others. One hand to her ear to block out the noise, she held the cell phone to her other ear. "Dr. Pulaski."

"Are you up to taking on another shift?" the voice on the other end of the line asked. She didn't have to ask who it was. She recognized Mark Howell's crisp, precise enunciation. The chief attending's speech was as neat as his work in the E.R. He also didn't wait for an answer before adding, "Two doctors called in sick."

Of course they did, Tania thought. To be fair, there was a particularly strong strain of flu making the rounds. "When do you want me?"

"Now would be good." His tone indicated that the conversation was a formality and that he expected her to comply.

Tania longed for the day when she was finally at the

top of the heap and her own boss. She began to doubt it would ever come. Biting back the sigh, she told Howell, "I'm on my way."

"I'll expect you." The line went dead.

Out of the corner of her eye, she saw Sasha looking in her direction. The moment she closed her phone, Sasha crossed to her. "I know you're indestructible, but shouldn't you get *some* rest?"

Yes, Tania thought, that had a nice sound to it, but she was the one who'd put her name down as backup for any no-shows in the E.R. So she forced a smile to her lips and said, "I take after Mama."

Sasha didn't back off. "That's when it comes to multitasking, not doing an imitation of some deranged mechanical bunny that never stops going. In case you don't remember, you don't run on batteries—and you just came off another one of your famous double shifts before you went out for dinner."

She knew Sasha meant well, but there were times when she felt everyone was looking over her shoulder, critiquing her life. "How would you know?" she asked. "You don't even live here anymore."

Sasha smiled as she unconsciously slipped her hand over her stomach. "I'm studying to be a mother, remember? Omniscient powers come with the territory. It's a package deal."

"Well, don't practice on me, okay?" And then, because she did know that Sasha was only looking out for her, Tania added, "Don't worry, if I get too tired, I'll take a cat nap."

"Just don't do it while you're sewing someone up," Kady deadpanned.

"Hey, she might do a better job that way," Marja pointed out.

Tania gave her a look before she went to her room. "That's enough out of you, Marja. You need to respect your elders."

"You're only my elder by thirteen months," Marja protested.

"And every second counts," Tania called back.

In her room, Tania went to her closet to get a change of clothing. Unlike her quandary while getting ready for Jesse, she pulled out the first two items that she came to, a navy-blue skirt and a light gray pullover. Less than ten minutes later, she was ready.

"Want to take the car?" Kady asked as Tania crossed the living room to the front door. "The car" was the one they all shared now that Sasha had moved out, taking hers with her.

Like the rest of her sisters, Tania had a driver's license. Unlike them, she was never completely comfortable behind the wheel. Her mind, so disciplined in the E.R., wandered too much when there was so much to look at. And besides, she grew impatient with the traffic that, at best, moved like petroleum jelly on a cold day.

So she shook her head in response to Kady's question. "It's a nice night, I think I'll just walk to the hospital."

Mike, Tony and Byron all exchanged glances and rose to their feet, propelled by the same thought. Tony and Byron put it into the exact same words almost simultaneously. "The hell you will."

Mike, the easier going of the three, grinned and jerked a thumb at the other two. "What they said, except maybe not so gruffly." He looked at Natalya. "You stay here with everyone. I'll be right back," he told his fiancée.

Natalya appreciated Mike's thoughtfulness. It wasn't something she'd take for granted anytime soon. "Looks like we've picked out good men," she said, addressing Kady and Sasha.

"Then hang on to them," Tania advised. She tried to beg off as politely as she could. "Really—" as she talked, she made her way to the door "—I just want to stretch my legs, maybe do a little thinking."

But Mike wasn't about to stay behind. The Pulaski women were all headstrong, but he'd been raised with sisters and he was not about to be talked out of what he knew was right.

"I won't interfere with your thoughts," Mike promised her, following her out the door. "But I'm not taking no for an answer, either."

Mike walked her to the elevator.

"You know, I am a big girl now," Tania told him as they rode down together to the first floor. "Been crossing the street by myself and everything ever since I was five years old."

He put his hand out to keep the doors open as he waited for her to walk out first. A second later he fell into step beside her.

"Knowing your mother, it was probably closer to eight, not five," Mike guessed, his voice easygoing. "You remind me a lot of one of my sisters," he continued. "Everyone else would say white, Gina would say 'black' just to stir things up and be different."

Where was this edginess coming from? she demanded of herself. He was just trying to be nice to her.

She should be grateful that Natalya was marrying such a good guy, not sulking because she couldn't be alone. Alone wasn't a good thing, she reminded herself. When she was alone, thoughts would come crowding into her head. Memories she didn't want, blocking out the myriad memories that were good.

"I'm not trying to be different. Or difficult," she added, guessing what might be crossing his mind. "I'm just trying not to inconvenience anyone."

In the basement, he led her toward where he had left his car in guest parking. Mike spread his hands wide. "Do I look inconvenienced?"

No, he didn't. He also wasn't quite as easygoing as he pretended, she thought. Her sister's marriage was going to be an interesting one.

"You look like a man who's going to spend a lot of time locking horns with Natalya. You know—" she waited for him to unlock her side "—Nat's not as easygoing as she might have led you to believe."

"Believe me, 'easygoing' was never a word I would have associated with your sister." He grinned. "Besides—" he put his key into the ignition and turned it "—a little bit of friction is what makes life interesting."

She glanced behind her as he pulled the car out of the parking spot. She thought she saw a movement out of the corner of her eye. Someone running. But when she looked, there was no one there. Maybe she *was* too tired, like Sasha said.

"Maybe not," she agreed absently. "But you know, you really don't have to go out of your way like this."

"The sooner I drop you off at the hospital, the sooner I'll be back," he pointed out.

She nodded. "I guess I can't argue with that."

He laughed, guiding the car out into the street. "That would be a first in your family."

Chapter 7

The light at the corner turned green. Tania went with the flow, working her way across the busy street. Even at seven-thirty in the morning, the streets and sidewalks were crammed with traffic, both vehicular and human.

She couldn't shake the feeling that she was being watched.

As she walked, she looked around. No one stood out, no one made eye contact. Just the opposite, if anything. The feeling refused to go away. Tania told herself that it was just her old paranoia revisiting her. She could feel the hairs standing up at the back of her neck.

Maybe she was just going crazy.

Granted, Jeff had been paroled recently and there was a part of her that worried he might try to make contact with her, might want to avenge himself because of the years she'd supposedly cost him.

But that would only put him back in jail. As part of his parole, he was supposed to stay far away from her. Her father had seen to that. And Jeff had sounded sincere at his allocution years ago, rendered just before he'd gone to prison. He'd apologized for the anguish and bodily harm he'd caused her. He'd blamed it on alcohol consumption, saying that none of it would have happened if he hadn't gotten drunk.

Of course, that had all been part of the bargain for a reduced sentence, his allocution and the fact that she didn't have to go through the gut-wrenching ordeal of a trial where she would have had to tell and retell her story before a courtroom full of strangers.

Jeff had been out for several months. Why was this uneasiness descending over her now?

Because her life was being shaken up, she thought. Shaken up for the first time since she'd consciously pulled her emotions out of the game, sealing them away. It was all Jesse's fault. Jesse and that damned hot mouth of his.

She enjoyed physical contact up to a point, but not to the degree where she'd lose herself, lose the ability to think clearly and function. For more than just a split second, when Jesse'd kissed her at her door, her mind had gone blank and her body had grown hot. As for the longing—well, she just didn't do that, didn't "long" for lovemaking.

And yet…

He'd made her long, made her want.

No wonder she was paranoid, Tania thought, annoyed. Jesse had thrown a huge monkey wrench into her life. She couldn't allow that to happen. From now on, she just needed to concentrate on her work and *nothing else.* God knew that was more than enough to keep any two people occupied.

Coming to the end of another block, Tania waited for the light to turn green and the Walk sign to beckon her forward.

She was walking to work, not exactly by choice but necessity. The bus she normally took when one of her sisters wasn't driving in at the same time she was due at the hospital had broken down and the one sent in to take its place, the driver had informed them, was running late. There'd all but been a mutiny as all the passengers got off the grounded bus.

Instead of waiting for another bus, Tania opted to walk off some of her nervous energy. The hospital really wasn't all that far. The sky above her was ominous with dark gray, pregnant clouds. She could almost smell the rain, but for now the air was heavy with oppressive humidity that seeped its way into everything. Running late, Tania had left the apartment without taking an umbrella.

Mentally she crossed her fingers that she'd reach Patience Memorial before the rain finally began to come down.

Waiting at yet another corner, Tania glanced to her right and thought she saw a long-range camera lens emerging from the driver's side of a car stopped at the light. The car had tinted windows so she couldn't look in to see the driver. Just the camera.

Her heart jumped. The camera was pointed in her direction.

It's a tourist, idiot, she upbraided herself. Probably some native from a tiny town in Montana whose entire population could fit on any New York street corner with room to spare.

The city could be overwhelming to people unaccustomed to the street's crowds at any given time of day or night.

So why did it feel as if the damn lens was focused on her?

Because you're overwrought and tired and your imagination is running away with you, she silently insisted. Just as it had the other day when someone had accidentally bumped into her, sending her off the curb and into the path of an oncoming bus. If someone else hadn't quickly grabbed her arm and pulled her back, she had no doubt that she would have found herself spending time in the hospital on the other side of the guardrail.

Tania picked up her pace. Even as she did, a fat raindrop fell directly on her head.

Terrific.

The car with the camera lens kept pace with her.

Drawing some of the oppressive air into her lungs, Tania wove her way through the crowd, moving faster. Four more long city blocks to go.

All the while, out of the corner of her eye, she continued to watch the car.

To her relief, the car disappeared at the end of the next block.

See? You're worried about nothing.

Her nervous feeling refused to retreat into the shadows.

Tania stripped off her surgical mask and took a deep breath. What a difference a few hours made.

She'd arrived at the hospital wet—it had rained for

the last block—with her nerves close to the surface. And then her current attending, Dr. Thomas Benedict, had asked her if she wanted to assist in what he whimsically referred to as a "simple procedure." It was a kyphoplasty. Her very first.

In essence the operation was a cousin to an angioplasty, except that it concerned itself with the spine rather than the heart. It entailed making a cut in the groin and snaking a wire up to the spinal area where, in this case, two balloons were inserted, one in each section where the patient had a minor spinal fracture. The balloons moved the spine back to its original position and then bone cement was squeezed into the newly created spaces to make the restoration permanent.

Under Benedict's watchful eye, Tania had inserted the cement, as well as closed up the initial incision. She left the operating room feeling as if she walked on air. The power to help, to heal, was an exceedingly heady sensation. It was like nothing else she'd ever experienced.

If, at dark times, she doubted herself, doubted the wisdom of her choices, being in the operating room lay those doubts to rest.

Surgery gave her a purpose, an identity.

Walking through the operating room's swinging doors, she leaned against the wall and savored the feeling.

One of the surgical nurses came out behind her. The woman raised her eyes as the P.A. system went off. She glanced at Tania. "Are you going to answer that?"

Tania blinked, realizing that she'd temporarily slipped into her own little world. She straightened, standing away from the wall. "Excuse me?"

The older woman pointed up in the general direction of the loudspeaker. "You're being paged."

Tania focused, listening. The woman over the P.A. said her name and asked her to pick up the nearest phone.

"Oh, right, I am. Thanks." She flashed a grin at the nurse and hurried over to the first interhospital wall phone she could find. "This is Dr. Tania Pulaski. You paged me?"

"You have a call," the operator told her. "Would you like me to put it through?"

"Sure, go ahead." She noticed a few of the hospital staff glancing in her direction as they went toward the elevator bank. Probably because she couldn't stop smiling, Tania thought.

"Go ahead, please," the operator said. Whether it was to her or whoever was on the other end of the line, Tania didn't know.

"This is Dr. Tania Pulaski," she repeated, turning to face the wall. It gave her the illusion of privacy.

"Finally," she heard the deep male voice on the other end say.

Tania felt an immediate, involuntary reaction. Her pulse accelerated. "Jesse?"

"You recognize my voice. I'm flattered."

She hadn't heard from him in three days and had begun to think that she wouldn't. "I'll call you" was such a throwaway line. Her smile widened. "Why are you calling me at the hospital?"

"Because your home number's unlisted and you never gave me your cell number."

She realized he was right. Self-preservation? "I didn't, did I?"

"You know," he told her, his voice deliberately lofty,

"if I wasn't as secure as I am, I'd say you were trying to avoid me."

Tania felt her mouth curving and told herself she was just still riding high from her OR experience. "Good thing you're so secure," she agreed.

"Listen, this hero thing has a few perks attached to it. The theater manager at the Schubert is somehow related to Mr. Epstein, the jewelry store owner. A nephew or second cousin, twice removed, something like that. Anyway, he called to tell me that there would be theater tickets waiting for me at the box office if I wanted to use them."

Tania's eyes widened. "For *Colors of the Rainbow?*"

The theater wasn't his thing and he wasn't sure if she had the right name. "I think that's the name of the play he mentioned."

She'd tried unsuccessfully to buy a pair of tickets for her parents. "That's the hottest musical in town," she told him. "The show is sold out for the next nine months."

"Since you know that, I take it that you like musicals."

She could hear his smile over the phone. "It's my guilty pleasure," she freely admitted. Her father had taken her to her first Broadway musical when she was ten. It was a Wednesday matinee on a two-fer ticket. He'd called in sick in order to take her to the play. She'd fallen in love that afternoon and had adored musicals ever since.

"Then would you like to go with me? It's for a week from Thursday night." He paused as he realized that he really didn't know her hours. "Unless you're on duty."

She was scheduled for the night shift on Thursdays until the end of the month, but that didn't daunt her.

"I can find someone to switch with." She said it as if it were a done deal. She'd put in so much extra time covering for other people, Tania was fairly certain that she could get someone to take her shift. If need be, she'd bribe someone.

"Great. I'll pick you up at your place at five-thirty."

That sounded pretty early. "Doesn't the show start at seven-thirty?"

"Yes," he answered. "But I thought I'd wine and dine you first."

What was the harm in that? she thought. As long as she knew what was ahead, she was prepared and could call the shots. And she *did* want to see the play. "You do know how to show a girl a good time."

"I do my best."

Tania could almost feel his words traveling along her skin and it took effort for her not to let herself drift with the sound of his voice. She abruptly changed the subject.

"Say, what's this I hear about you turning down an interview on *The Today Show?*"

"Not my thing, remember?"

Because she liked to fill the apartment with sound when she was alone, Tania always turned on the TV set in the living room. She'd caught part of the local heroes segment before she hurried out the door this morning. "Maybe you should have made an exception this time. They had Mr. Epstein on in your place and to hear him tell it, Joshua storming the walls of Jericho was a wimp in comparison to you. I think he just drummed up another fifteen minutes of fame for you."

She heard Jesse sigh. "I keep hoping this'll all blow over."

"It will." Everything always did. "But in the meantime," she reminded him, "you do have those tickets to the hottest show in town."

She heard him laugh softly and the sound went straight to her stomach despite her efforts to block it. "Yes, I do. Which allows me to take out the hottest woman in town. See you next Thursday."

Tania ran her tongue along her extradry lips. "See you."

Hanging up the receiver, Tania stood where she was for a second, trapped in the excited moment.

"I heard you just assisted in your very first kyphoplasty. Congratulations." Coming to, Tania turned to see Sasha approaching. "By the way, did that candy striper ever find you?"

Tania forced herself to focus. Was it her imagination or was Sasha looking thinner these days? "What candy striper?"

"I guess she didn't, then," Sasha surmised. "Just some candy striper who wanted to know where to find you earlier. I said you were in surgery."

Tania shook her head. She couldn't imagine why one of the volunteers would be searching for her. Maybe whoever it was had her confused with one of her sisters. That seemed the more likely scenario.

"Did she say what she wanted?"

"Not to me, although I did tell her you were my sister so I'd pass any message along if she wanted me to. But she said that was okay."

Mildly curious, Tania asked, "Did she give you a name?"

"No, but she had 'Carol' sewn on her blouse." Sasha

began to walk toward the elevator banks. Tania fell into step with her. "Funny thing, though, when I called her that, she didn't respond right away."

Tania didn't see anything unusual in that. "Okay, so Patience Memorial doesn't attract rocket scientists as volunteers." She shrugged. "I guess whatever she wanted to tell me couldn't have been all that important, otherwise she would have left a message in my in-box."

Sasha nodded as she pressed for the up elevator. "How long are you going to keep grinning?"

Tania thought of the operation she'd just assisted with—and the phone call from Jesse. Her grin grew. "Not sure. A while. Why, does it bother you?"

Sasha's eyes crinkled as she smiled back at her little sister. "No, just reminds me how much I miss seeing you look like that. Happy."

Just like Mama, Tania thought. "I'm happy, Sasha."

An elevator dinged, then opened, but it was going down to the basement. Sasha pressed the up button again. "It wouldn't have anything to do with that guy you were kissing the other evening, would it?"

"Kissed, not kissing," Tania corrected. Sasha had been the only one who hadn't come to the door the other night. "'Kissing' implies something that was ongoing. He just kissed me good-night."

Sasha shook her head. "Not to hear Nat tell it. She said the two of you were so sealed together, not even air could have slipped in between you."

Tania sighed. Privacy was not a viable word in her family. "Natalya exaggerates."

"If you say so, kid." Sasha's tone indicated that she was more inclined to believe Natalya over her protest.

The up elevator finally arrived. "Well, I have a baby to usher into the world. I'll see you tonight at Mom and Dad's," she said, stepping into the car.

"Oh, dinner." Tania caught her lower lip in her teeth. "I forgot."

The doors began to close and Sasha put her hand in the way, causing them to spring back. "I kinda thought you might. This is the push to get Mama to start up her own business—and back away a little from ours."

"I'll be there with bells on," Tania promised as the doors closed again.

Josef Pulaski sat at the head of the dining-room table, hands placed on either side of his plate, his eyes all but disappearing as he smiled broadly in deep, nostalgic satisfaction. All five of his daughters were present, along with his son-in-law, his two sons-in-law-to-be, as well as his much beloved wife. If there was any man who was more fortunate than he was, Josef wanted to meet him.

"Ah, all five of my girls sitting at my table at the same time. It is making me remember when they were all young," he said to Byron who sat closest to him.

"We still are young, Daddy," Natalya corrected. "The word you're looking for is 'younger.'"

"No." Josef sighed dramatically—years with Magda had rubbed off on him. "The word is old. I am getting old. Old, and my babies are getting married, getting babies, too."

"Baby," Kady interjected with feeling. She'd made it clear she wanted children, but not immediately. "There's only one in the immediate future."

"But there will be more babies, yes?" Josef looked hopefully at all three of the men seated around him at the table.

Mike laughed. "Hey, if it were up to me, you'd have a houseful—and soon."

"Houseful, huh?" Natalya's eyes went from Mike to Byron to Tony and then back to the culprit. "And you men can take care of them."

Josef took the words at face value and beamed. "Now that is what I want to be hearing. I will be watching them for all of you," he promised.

Sitting at the other end of the table, Magda made a small, dismissive sound as she waved away her husband's words. "Like you watched Marja when she put all those fuzzy plants into her nose?"

Marja cringed. "The pussy willow story again."

Josef rolled his eyes and looked at the three men at the table for empathy. "One time." He held up his index finger. "One time I am looking away, watching baseball game, and this one—" he waved a hand at Marja "—is breaking my record as a good father."

"Can we move on, please?" Marja pleaded.

"All right," her mother allowed magnanimously. "Tony, have some more of my dessert," she urged her son-in-law. It was a golden bundt cake made with wine and drizzled with melted powdered sugar and more wine. As Sasha reached for one of the sliced pieces herself, Magda drew the dessert back. "Not you, Sasha. You do not want the baby to get too much wine."

"Alcohol evaporates when you bake," Sasha reminded her mother, and then she exchanged looks with Kady and Natalya. It was time.

Natalya rose to the occasion. "Mama, we've been thinking you need a hobby."

Magda looked put off. "What 'hobby'? I have your father. I have all of you—and the baby. I have no time for this 'hobby.'"

Undaunted, Kady put in her two cents' worth. "We were thinking of a catering company."

Magda frowned. They had danced this dance before once or twice. She loved to cook, but to charge for that cooking was another matter. "That is not a hobby, that is a business."

"Wouldn't you want your own business?" Sasha asked, trying to sound supportive.

"I have my own business," Magda insisted. She gestured around the table. "Family—this is my business."

"We're going around in circles," Tania pointed out to her sisters.

"Yes, we are," Magda agreed. "So, we step out of that circle," she declared, then turned intent hazel eyes on Tania. "How is that new young man?"

Josef looked from his wife to Tania and then back again. He was obviously not happy about being out of the loop. "What new young man? There is a new young man?"

"No," Tania said firmly.

"Yes," Magda contradicted. "The hero," she informed her husband. "The one who stopped that thief. In the paper," she said with exasperation when Josef continued to eye her blankly. "I showed you."

Josef's eyebrows drew together to form one wavy, gray line. "She is seeing a hero? Why am I not knowing about this?"

"You are knowing about it now, Josef," Magda said, slipping another piece of cake on his plate.

It was going to be a very long night, Tania thought, bracing herself.

Chapter 8

"You know, maybe I'll just elope," Natalya muttered as she stood outside the rear E.R. doors beside Tania.

She'd sought out her younger sister a few minutes ago, opting to take Tania's break with her before going back up to her own office. The sigh that followed sounded as if it came from her very toes.

"All these plans, all these choices, it's just driving me crazy. I've been so busy, I haven't seen Mike in three days, not since dinner at Mom and Dad's. But somehow, whether I want to or not, I've managed to see Mama every day. She keeps popping up like toast." Natalya flashed a semicontrite smile that was gone the next instant. "Not that I don't love her, but—"

Tania didn't need to hear the disclaimer. They all loved Mama, but they all knew she could be a bit much at times. However, there was no getting away from a few simple facts. Tania pinned her sister with a look.

"You elope and Mama's going to have heart failure. And you *know* you'll have that on your conscience for the rest of your natural life."

"I'll tell her with Kady around." Kady was the heart specialist in the family. "If anyone can bring Mama back from the dead, it's Kady." And then she surrendered with another deep sigh. "Don't give me that look. I know, I'm only talking. I'll go through with this three-ring circus." Natalya shoved her hands deep into the pockets of her crisp lab coat. "I just think it's too much of a fuss. Who cares what kind of flowers are used as the centerpieces?"

"Mama does," Tania replied simply. She ran her hands along her arms and glanced up at the less than blue sky. More rain was coming. "What does Mike think about all this?"

Natalya smiled at the mention of her fiancé's name. "Mike comes from a large Italian family. He's used to mothers fussing over nonsense."

Tania thought someday Natalya was going to look back at all this organized chaos and laugh. But probably not anytime soon. For a second she found herself envying her older sister for having found someone so understanding. She really liked the police detective who was joining the family. "Lucky for you."

"Yeah," Natalya agreed, echoing the sentiment. "Lucky for me."

"You have that goofy grin on again," Tania teased.

"It is *not* a goofy grin," Natalya said defensively, then relented just a little. "Wait'll you fall in love, Tania. You'll see."

As far as Tania was concerned, it was a promise without foundation.

"Maybe," Tania said carelessly.

She sincerely doubted she would ever be in that position, ever find anyone she wanted to love. And even if she did, even if she met someone absolutely perfect in every way—and what chance was there of that?—opening up to someone wouldn't be easy for her, if not impossible. A part of her was completely blocked off inside, unreachable.

But there was no point in discussing it. So Tania humored her sister and agreed. She winced as she heard the squeal of brakes in the distance. But it wasn't followed by the sound of metal meeting metal and the tension left her shoulders.

Tania glanced at her watch. "Looks like my break's over." She turned toward the rear doors. "Time to get back to work."

Natalya stopped leaning against the wall. "Yeah, me, too." She hurried inside and turned left, heading toward the back elevators. "See you later."

"Think honeymoon," Tania called after her.

"It's the only thing keeping me sane," Natalya assured her as she walked quickly to the elevator bank.

The moment she walked back into the E.R. area, one of the nurses handed Tania a file. There was a broad grin on her face as she did so.

Tania raised an inquiring eyebrow.

"Mr. Wonderful is back," the young woman told her. There was a hint of a sigh attached to the statement.

"Excuse me?" Tania glanced at the file for some edification.

The nurse gave Tania the answer before she had a chance to read the name neatly typed across the tab. "That hunk that made the newspapers. By the way, he asked for you." There was envy in the nurse's brown eyes. "Room five," she added, needlessly nodding in the trauma room's direction.

File in hand, Tania quickly made her way to the last trauma room.

She didn't like the way her pulse quickened for a second, wasn't happy that anticipation suddenly surged in her chest. And certainly wasn't thrilled by the way her heart all but leaped up when she pushed open the door and Jesse looked in her direction, their eyes meeting.

She wasn't supposed to feel any of these things. Wasn't supposed to feel, period..

"Been tackling another thief?" she asked, coming closer and opening the file.

It wasn't his imagination, Jesse thought. She *was* gorgeous. Even more than he remembered. "No."

She placed the folder on the side counter. "Then to what do we owe the pleasure of your company?"

My God, that sounded as if it had come out of a grade-B movie straight out of the seventies, Tania berated herself. What the hell was the matter with her? She didn't talk like that.

A smattering of confusion brought his eyebrows together. "You told me to come, remember? Follow-up care," he prompted when she gave no indication that she knew what he was talking about.

Embarrassment kissed her cheeks, giving them a very inviting, pink hue. He caught himself wanting to rub his thumb along her cheek, to lightly trace the path of the color as it made its way up her skin.

"I can come back if you're too busy," he offered.

"No, there's no point in that. We're always busy," she said quickly.

God, but she felt like an idiot, forgetting those very basic instructions. Seeing him had knocked all logic out of her head. For a split second, she'd thought that maybe he'd come just to see her.

Why should that even matter?

It didn't, she insisted silently.

Doing her best to seem all business, she paused to slip on a pair of gloves. "How have you been doing?" she asked. "Any headaches, blurred vision—" she drew closer to him "—dizziness?"

As she leaned forward to examine a bruise, he took in a deep breath, letting the scent of her perfume filter into his senses.

"Maybe a little dizziness," he allowed.

Tania drew back to look at him, concerned. "When?"

His smile hit her right in the pit of her stomach, causing a minor tidal wave. "Whenever I'm around you," he told her innocently.

"Oh, that kind of dizziness." She gave him a knowing look. "The flirting kind." She lightly touched another, larger bruise at the side of his neck. "I'm talking about the serious kind."

"Then no, no dizziness." She stepped away for a moment and he twisted around to watch her. "You know, I don't really do this sort of thing."

"Flirt?" Her mouth curved with amusement. "I find that hard to believe."

"No, go to a doctor, especially for something like 'follow-up care.'" He'd grown up without any health care of any kind and learned to tough things out for the most part.

She paused a moment, her eyes meeting his. He was just too damn good-looking. How she tried vainly to maintain proper boundaries. "Then why did you?"

Jesse had a feeling that honesty was the best way to go with her. "Because I wanted to see you again and a follow-up seemed like a good excuse. You know," he pointed out, "if you were a gnarled old man, I wouldn't be here right now."

Tania couldn't help smiling. "So this is all my fault."

He nodded solemnly, but his eyes gave him away. "That's the way I see it."

She took a disinfectant out of the overhead cabinet, just in case. "But you are going to see me again," she reminded him. "The play next Thursday." She stopped as the thought occurred to her. "Or is that off?"

"No, that's very much on." He barely felt her fingers as she gently examined the area around his stitches. "Listen, can you get away for a cup of coffee? I told them at the firm that I wouldn't be back until after lunch, sometime around one. That gives me a least an hour to kill."

"And you want to kill some time with me?"

She sounded amused, he thought, grateful that she hadn't taken his statement the wrong way. "That didn't come out right, did it?"

He heard her laugh. "At least I know you're not the type who hands out lines. Unless this tripping-over-your-own-tongue is really just a bit."

Her lab coat brushed against his face as she examined another scrape. "Not very trusting, are you?"

No, she thought, trust was forfeited more than ten years ago. She finished and gazed down at him. "I'm a New Yorker, remember?"

Jesse studied her for a long moment. "No, I think it might be something more than that."

That he could see past the surface made her uncomfortable. "I thought you said you were an architect, not a psychiatrist." Stepping back, she removed the rubber gloves and then tossed them into the wastebasket. "Well, you look fine. The stitches are coming along nicely. No sign of infection. You won't be needing any more follow-up care," she told him. "Unless there's a problem."

This had gone much too quickly and he wasn't willing to give up her presence just yet. "Well, my first problem is that you won't have coffee with me."

She made a notation in his chart. An enigmatic smile played on her lips. "I didn't say I wouldn't."

"Then it's yes?"

Done with the chart, she flipped it closed. He was relieved to see humor in her eyes. "I didn't say that, either. I don't like being second-guessed."

He kept it light. "The question is, do you like coffee?"

What was it about this man that made her want to smile? She remembered Natalya's words about the goofy smile and waiting until it was her turn.

Just proved that her sister didn't know everything, Tania thought stubbornly. If she had a goofy smile, it had nothing to do with being in love, just being tickled and amused, that's all.

"Yes," she told him, "I like coffee."

"Then would you be willing to have a cup with me now?" he asked.

He was asking, not assuming. They were making progress.

"Better," she commented with a nod of her head. "But the answer's still no. I just had my break," she explained. "And we're full up here. So, Mr. Steele, if you don't have any further questions—"

Anticipating her departure, Jesse slid off the gurney to his feet. He grabbed the suit jacket he'd removed. "Oh, but I do. Lots of questions."

"Such as?"

Placing himself between her and the door, Jesse began to enumerate.

"What's your favorite color? Are you a morning person or an evening person? Do you prefer long walks on the beach or window-shopping on Fifth Avenue? What kind of movies do you prefer?" Jesse took in a breath. "Are you—"

"Wait, wait," she cried, laughing, raising her hands up to stop the torrent of words. "I meant questions about your condition."

He turned the word to his advantage. "This *is* about my condition," Jesse told her innocently. Taking one of her hands, he placed it across his chest. She could feel the beat of his heart beneath her fingertips. "My heart condition."

She rolled her eyes as she reclaimed her hand. "Oh, brother." Still laughing, she shook her head. "I take it back. You *do* have lines."

The grin on his lips slipped into a smile, a small, deep, heartfelt smile. "No, actually," he told her solemnly, "I don't. Nothing's tried and true here. I'm just saying what comes into my head." His eyes held hers. Something rippled inside her very core. "There's something going on here, Tania. An attraction I haven't felt in a long, long time." Since the episode with Ellen, he hadn't really trusted any of the women he'd come across. The few he had gone out with in the last six months had been interchangeable. But this was different. He could feel it in his bones and he needed to explore it further. "I'm hoping it's not one-sided."

Why couldn't she lie? Other people lied without effort. But she couldn't.

"No," she admitted with more than a little reluctance. "It's not."

He'd heard project bids rejected with more joy. "You don't sound very happy about it."

"I don't trust attractions, Jesse." It felt strange saying his name, strange removing that small, artificial barrier between them where he called her by her title and she used his surname. This was getting way too personal way too fast.

Jesse was silent for a moment and then he asked, "Relationship go sour?"

Too close, too close, her mind cried, sounding an alarm. "I don't know you well enough to tell you that," she said stiffly.

She needed boundaries, he could live with that. For now. "I'm willing to wait."

It was going to be a *very* long wait. She shrugged. "Suit yourself."

Damn, but he wanted to kiss her, to break through her reserve and get her to trust him. But he knew he couldn't.

Slow and steady, his mother used to say. "You know, you're a lot more complicated than you seem."

She raised her chin, not happy that he had her pegged so easily so quickly. "Life is more complicated than we're led to believe," she countered.

He didn't quite see it that way. "Not the important things. They're still relatively simple." Because he could see that he hadn't convinced her, he enumerated, "Love, loyalty, family."

Tania laughed despite herself. And then she shook her head. And where had she heard *that* before? "My father would love you."

The ex-policeman, he recalled. "I'd like to meet him."

Oh, no, she wasn't about to bring him around. She hadn't brought anyone around in ten years and it was staying that way. Her family was precious, this was just a diversion, albeit a good-looking one, but just a diversion, nothing more.

"You're getting ahead of yourself," she told him quietly.

He took no offense. Instead he agreed with her, in an effort to catch her off guard.

"I have that tendency," he admitted. "Part of my go-getter personality." And then he became serious again, just for a moment. "I won't hurt you, Tania."

Her response was glib. "I know." *Because I won't let you.*

He broke the tense moment with a laugh, dragging his hand through his hair, careful to avoid the area with the stitches. "Wow, this is a lot more serious than I intended to get." He slipped on his jacket and left it un-buttoned. "So, no coffee?"

He was tempting her more than she was happy about,

but she wasn't about to bend the rules over something as minor as an illegal break.

"No coffee."

Taking her answer in stride, he had a second request. "Walk me out?"

Did he never stop? "How long are you going to play the irresistible card?"

"As long as I can." In the corridor, he glanced around. To his left was the front of the hospital, to his right, the way he'd come in the first time, on a gurney. It was closer and far less busy. "Can I take the back way?"

Leaving was leaving. Tania shrugged. "Sure." And then, since everyone went out the front, curiosity got the better of her. "Why?"

"Because it's shorter and it gives me a shot at asking you to walk with me a little longer."

He *was* charming, she thought. And she needed to be on her guard. "I'm on duty."

He nodded, acknowledging her words with a solemn, straight face. "I know."

"That means I should be attending to other patients. *Real* patients," she emphasized in case he missed the obvious point.

"I am a real patient," he told her. "If you prick me, do I not bleed? If you kill me, do I not die?"

He was damn cute and he knew it. "Okay, okay, Shylock. I'll walk you—but just to the back exit." If he thought he could convince her to keep walking until they came to the coffee shop on the next block, he was in for a disappointment.

He spread his hands innocently, fighting the urge to slip an arm around her shoulder. "I'm not a demanding man."

"The hell you're not."

Tania walked beside him until they came to the rear doors. When they opened, she took a few steps outside. Going further than she knew she should. She was aware that they'd garnered more than a few glances as they passed some of the hospital staff.

Still his fifteen minutes of fame, she thought, amused.

"Okay, here we are, outside." She gestured about the opened area to underscore her point. "Now, off you go."

But he lingered. And the look in his eyes told her why. "One more thing."

"Of course there is." Resigned, she asked, "And that is?"

There was not a hint of a smile on his face as he said, "I'd like to kiss you. I normally don't believe in asking for permission, but with you, I have a feeling that I should."

A breeze of anxiety mingled with anticipation. This man was too damn intuitive for her own good, Tania thought. He was changing the rules and blurring the parameters. She desperately needed to be on top, to take charge.

So, instead of answering, Tania took his face in her hands, raised herself up on her toes and pressed her lips against his. The moment she did, the control she thought she'd just taken instantly slipped right through her fingers like water through a sieve.

Her head swirled.

It was just like the first time, except more. More exhilarating, more overwhelming, more exciting.

More.

Caught off guard, Tania leaned her body into his as the kiss continued to deepen. Her hands left his face and were now knotted around his neck, anchoring her because she was afraid of being swept out to sea.

Afraid of this kiss.

And more afraid of it ending.

The longing she'd felt the other night returned in spades, hot and demanding, and she was oh so grateful they were out here, in public, so that nothing could come of it. So that she couldn't give in to the urges that all but ravaged her.

There it was again, Jesse thought. The want. The need. Battering his body so that he could hardly stand it. He knew he had to break contact before he broke into a million little pieces.

Breathing heavily, he leaned his cheek against the top of her head, just holding her for a moment. Waiting for the fever to pass.

"I'm glad I asked," he finally said softly.

"Me, too," she murmured before she could stop herself. She was giving too much away, damn it.

He stepped back to look at her, reluctantly releasing her from his arms. "I'll see you next Thursday."

And with that, he turned on his heel and walked away. Quickly.

Aroused, shaken, confused, Tania stood to the side of the electronic E.R. doors, watching him go. Her insides were so jumbled, she didn't know where to begin to try to sort them out.

At the very least, she needed her heart to stop doing double-time.

Closing her eyes, she took a deep breath and let it out very slowly. When she opened her eyes again, she realized that she was experiencing that odd sensation again. The one that had her thinking someone was watching her.

She looked around, but there was no one there, no one visible.

Get a grip, she ordered herself.

Turning, she walked back through the electronic doors. A candy striper quickly moved out of her way.

"Sorry," the woman apologized.

Preoccupied, Tania merely nodded. "My fault," she murmured as she hurried back to the central desk.

Chapter 9

The state-of-the-art printer hummed loudly as the color ink-jets within it rhythmically passed back and forth over the four-by-six glossy paper being fed through its carriage.

Slowly the paper inched its way out of the mouth of the printer, displaying an image of two people kissing.

The moment the process was finished, she snatched the paper from the printer, tossing the newly minted photograph on top of the other photographs she'd just printed. The captured images formed an untidy little pile, all of which had been locked within the tiny, thin body of a memory stick.

Now those images were multiplying, emerging on paper and sealing themselves into the computer's hard drive where they would remain forever more.

Until rage or its kin made her delete them.

It wasn't that she was storing and producing the images for sentiment's sake.

Quite the opposite was true.

Sentiment had only been involved in the flattering photographs she'd taken of Jesse, the ones that made love to his face, to his body, or caught him in midaction, doing something noble, the way it had that day he'd come to the jeweler's aid.

There'd even been poetic images, thanks to the long-range lens she'd invested in. Images like the ones of Jesse being taken out of the ambulance and into the hospital. A hero in need of mending.

Those she'd printed up immediately. They joined the others, the hundreds of photographs both on her computer and in the score of albums she'd painstakingly put together. The albums that she'd sit and pore over, night after night. Looking and remembering.

And waiting.

But these photographs that the printer was now spitting out, the ones she planned to upload onto her hard drive, they served a different purpose.

They were to galvanize her into action, to make her remember that she couldn't become too complacent. To remind her that there was a threat and she had to be ready to deal with it.

Not some distant "someday," but soon.

Soon.

The printer finished producing yet another photograph. The one of Jesse kissing that slut outside the hospital. Her rage mounting to barely contained proportions, she reached for the photograph.

Soon.

* * *

It was a long time, years to be exact, since Tania had been governed by impulses. In the last ten, she'd become very didactic, very controlled when it came to her personal life away from the family.

So no one was more surprised than she when she heard herself saying yes to Jesse's impromptu invitation to dinner the next evening. Especially since the latter part of her evening wasn't free. She had things to do and promises to keep.

She was deviating from her normal pattern and it didn't make her happy. And yet the prospect of seeing Jesse, of sitting across from him at a table, with soft music in the background, made her pulse quicken and ushered in a feeling of anticipation.

Warning herself to be careful in no way tempered her reaction to him. She did what she could to put safeguards in place.

"This is going to have to be quick," she warned, vaguely aware that she was guilty of repeating herself. Nerves did that to her.

The restaurant turned out to be far from romantic. Located not far from her apartment and specializing in crepes, *Wraps* smiled upon families. The well-behaved kind. There were no children throwing tantrums or running in between the tables, but they were there nonetheless, displaying the true riches that life had to give.

"I know," Jesse replied mildly, "you told me." Being a gentleman, he didn't go on to say just how many times she had told him. He would have said that she really didn't want to be here, but that wasn't what her eyes were telling him.

Still, he sensed tension from her and wasn't sure what to make of it. But tension or not, he liked being around her. Each time he saw her, he became more and more aware of that.

"I promise not to tie you up and toss you into my car after dinner," he assured her, a smile playing on his lips. He raised his eyes from his dinner. "Would I be out of line if I asked why this has to be quick?"

He wasn't challenging her, Tania realized, he was being understanding and putting up with her various quirks.

Mama would have said to grab the man and run. But while involving scores of hardships, Mama's history did not come close to equaling the trauma that she had gone through. Mama's travails had not taken her young, trusting optimism and shattered it into a million pieces by having her suffer betrayal at the hands of someone she'd regarded as a friend.

Regarded as more than that.

With effort, Tania managed a smile, trying very hard to banish the darker feelings that kept trying to surface.

"Yes, you can ask." Amusement curved her mouth. "And I'll even answer you. I have to meet my sisters and mother at a bridal shop." She saw him raise an eyebrow in a silent query. "Two of my sisters are getting married. We were going to have two separate ceremonies, but now the idea of a double wedding is being bandied about." She remembered her father's response when the idea was broached. "Daddy calls it killing two crows with a rock." She grinned. "Daddy and the English language are not always all that compatible. But he does try."

"A double wedding is cost-efficient," Jesse allowed. Although, when it came to the big day, he wasn't sure if he would want to share the occasion with someone other than his bride-to-be.

She took a sip of the drink, thinking of the last spate of "disagreements" that had taken place over pending wedding plans. "Nerve efficient is more like it."

Her choice of words intrigued him. "You're going to have to explain that."

Tania looked at him for a long moment. "My mother," was all she said. All she felt she needed to say. She didn't want to sit here and spend her time complaining about the kindest, most loving woman in the world. Jesse didn't know her mother and he might get the wrong idea. However, Magda Pulaski was not perfect and there were times when her forceful personality did get under everyone's skin in one way or another.

Except for her husband.

Josef Pulaski was a saint when it came to tolerating his wife's various quirks. A marriage that had obviously been made in heaven. Too bad so many marriages were made here on earth instead.

Jesse nodded as if he knew exactly what she meant. "I hear a lot of mothers of the bride and the groom— terrific women normally—go off the deep end when a wedding's involved."

Yes, she thought, Mama would definitely love this man. "Mama never had anything fancy when she got married. A bouquet of flowers Daddy picked for her from the field. They said their vows before a priest and a couple of witnesses, that was all," Tania told him. "So I guess she's trying to make up for it with us." There was affection in her voice when she said, "I think she was planning weddings from the minute each of us was born." She grinned. "Natalya keeps threatening to run off to city hall and elope if Mama doesn't tone things down. It kind of helps rein Mama in." She saw the amused expression on his face. He leaned forward, as if trying to absorb every word she said. "What? Did I just say something funny?"

"No, I just like hearing you talk about your family, that's all." He drew himself back a little. "Sounds like you all really love each other."

"We do," she said simply. And then she remembered something he'd told her before. "That's right, you don't have any siblings." Despite the fact that there were occasions when she wanted to be alone, being an only child sounded awfully lonely. He had to have somebody. "How about cousins?"

He shook his head, his face impassive. "As far as I know, both my parents were only children."

She could almost *feel* the emptiness. Her heart went out to him before she could stop it. "Christmas must be very tame around your place."

"So tame that sometimes it goes completely unnoticed."

"Oh." There was a great deal of pain and compassion packed into the single, one-syllable word. So much so that it made him smile.

He shrugged carelessly. It had been a long time since this was of any consequence to him. "I've gotten used to it."

She shook her head. "That's not anything to get used to," she said firmly. And then suddenly, impulse took over before she could head it off at the pass. "You're invited to our place for Christmas—and by that, I mean my parents' house," she clarified. "It's where all of us celebrate the holidays. Wouldn't really seem right anywhere else," she confided. And then she realized how Jesse might interpret the invitation. As if she were making plans for the future. *Their* future. "I don't mean to imply that you and I will still be seeing each other by then—"

"Out of sheer curiosity," he interrupted her, his voice low, intrigued, "why wouldn't we?"

She evaded the question, offering only a vague answer. "I never plan my social life that far ahead—and most men I know don't, either," she added with feeling. "I didn't mean to give you the impression that I think of us as a couple." She was sinking badly. "I just don't want you to have to be alone during the holidays."

"That's very nice of you," he acknowledged and then, after mulling it over a beat, asked, "What do you think of us as?"

She'd decided it was safer to focus her attention for the remainder of the meal *on* her meal. Obviously he wasn't going to let her. "Excuse me?"

"You said that you didn't think of us as a couple, so I was just curious how you did think of us. Two ships passing in the night?" he suggested helpfully.

"Not passing. Not yet," she qualified, then added, "Maybe two ships docked at the same harbor for a stretch of time."

Finished with his meal, Jesse moved the plate aside. She felt as if he was peeling away barriers. "That's very antiseptic sounding. I don't feel very antiseptic when I'm around you," he told her quietly. "And you certainly don't kiss antiseptically." He paused for a moment, as if searching for something. She felt as if he was looking right through her. "What are you afraid of, Tania?"

Tania's chin shot up as she pulled her shoulders back. She looked like a soldier about to go into battle.

"Nothing," she retorted. "I'm afraid of nothing."

"Ah, fearless." He nodded, playing along.

His gut instincts told him that her answer had been triggered by some sort of defense mechanism. He intended to get her story, but knew that it wasn't just going to come pouring out. Certainly not here at the table. Probably not soon, either.

Jesse understood secrets, understood the self-preserving need to have them and the need, eventually, to share them. They weren't at that point yet—at least she wasn't, but something told him that they would be. Eventually. Just because he'd told her about Ellen the other day didn't necessarily mean that she was going to show him the skeletons in her closet.

But he knew she had them as surely as he knew his own name. "I find that very sexy in a woman—being fearless—as long as you don't try to catch bullets with your bare hands," he teased.

She felt uneasy, as if he could read her thoughts the moment that she formed them. It was a ridiculous notion and yet…

Tania changed the subject, turning the conversation around so that it was about him for a change and not her. She needed the respite.

"So, tell me about your work," she asked, her tone mild, coaxing. She knew how to play the dating game if she had to. "Would I have seen any of your buildings in the city?"

Jesse grinned. He could have lied to her if he wanted, make himself seem more important than he was, but he never saw the point in that. It took the edge off triumph when it finally did arrive.

"I haven't been in the game long enough to 'have a building,'" he told her. "However, bits and pieces of my contributing designs have turned up in a few edifices currently going up."

It seemed to Tania that the city was continuously under construction. It was hard to walk any distance in any direction within New York City, especially in Manhattan, without finding some building going up or being torn down so another could be put up in its place.

"Eventually," he was saying, "if the firm continues to be happy with me and likes my input, there may someday be a building I can point to and claim as mine."

Someday. Which was a time beyond Christmas. Beyond the scope of anything she intended to think about. It almost took her breath away. A kind of panic threatened to overtake her. There were no "somedays" for her, at least, not when it came to male companionship. There was only "now," only the present. Tomorrow wasn't something to be contemplated.

So why did what he had just said frighten and thrill her at the same time?

Her head began to ache. He confused her, scrambled her brain, and she didn't like it. Didn't like not having a clear head. This couldn't go on. She would have to come up with a better defense strategy, not just against him, but against herself, as well.

Because from where she stood, she was inching over to his side.

Just for the time being. Just for fun, nothing more.

Tania drew in a breath. Her plate was clean, her drink consumed, and the minutes were ticking away fast. She needed to get going in order to reach her mother's friend's shop on time. It was the same store where Sasha had bought her wedding dress. Mama's friend had promised to close the bridal shop this evening so that Natalya and Kady could take as much time as they needed to look around and make their decisions without interference.

Without interference. Well, for that to happen, she mused, Mama would have to be locked out.

Tania needed to get going. For more reasons than one.

Wiping her fingers, she tossed her napkin on top of her silverware and prepared to evacuate. Quickly, before reluctance got the better of her.

"I'm afraid I have to eat and run," she apologized, moving back her chair.

Leaning forward, he caught her wrist. She looked at him quizzically, debating whether or not she would need to make a scene.

"Well, you've eaten," he said, "but in all good conscience, I can't let you run."

Okay, here it comes, Tania thought, her own reluctance instantly disappearing. He was going to try to talk her into lingering. She knew he'd been too good to be true.

"I told you," she reminded him evenly, her free hand gathering her purse to her, "I have to meet my mother and sisters at the bridal shop."

"I know, I remember our conversation this afternoon." Still holding her by the wrist, Jesse raised his other hand to get the waiter's attention. The young man spotted him and smiled obligingly. Jesse mouthed, "Check, please."

With a nod of his head, the waiter went to get their meal's final tally.

"Then what is all this about your conscience?" she asked.

"My car's in the lot across the street," he reminded her. He'd driven them over from her apartment rather than use a taxi. "I'm not about to have you run, take the bus or the subway, to this shop. There's no point in my having a car in the city if I can't drive you where you have to go."

There was something flawed in that, but she couldn't put her finger on just what. She opened her mouth to argue the point and discovered that she really didn't want to. Moreover, the thought of more time with Jesse tempted her.

She wondered if twenty-nine was too young to be losing her mind.

Tania tried to appeal to his sense of logic, although a man who chased after a thief with a gun couldn't be the most logical resident in the building. "Are you sure you want to put up with city traffic at this time?"

In his opinion, anytime was a bad time for city traffic. "Whether I take you to the shop or go home, I still have to put up with the traffic," he pointed out. And then he smiled. "I might as well be doing a good deed."

There it was again, that disarming smile that sliced through everything like a rapier, leaving her damn near defenseless. She surrendered gracefully. "All right then, thank you."

He released her wrist and rose, as did she. For a split

second, their bodies almost collided. Jesse stepped back, giving her room.

"You're welcome."

The waiter arrived, their receipt poised in his hand. Jesse had had his credit card run through when he'd initially ordered drinks for them so it was merely a matter of signing the slip of paper after adding in the tip.

Rather than write an amount in, Jesse dug into his pocket for his wallet. He handed the waiter what came to a little more than twenty percent of their bill in cash. The young man stared at the windfall before stammering a thank-you and hurrying away.

Tania eyed the man beside her. "Why did you do that?" she asked as he held the outside door open for her.

Once she was across the threshold, he followed her out. "Do what?"

For once, the humidity seemed manageable. Thank God for small favors, she thought. "Give the waiter cash instead of adding the amount to the credit card slip?"

"This way, if things are very, very tight, he doesn't have to claim it."

She glanced at him, remembering times that had been "very, very tight" for her family. Her parents would have welcomed a helping hand like that. Still, she played it straight. "So you're advocating fraud?"

He couldn't tell by her expression if she was serious. He could only tell her the truth. "I'm advocating compassion and bending the rules a little. Besides, who's to say I didn't just give him a loan instead of a tip? That is possible, right?"

"Right." Tania couldn't hold back any longer. "You are a nice man, Jesse Steele."

"That's what I've been trying to tell you," he said solemnly, then grinned. "Okay, let's go. You can help me find my car."

He placed his hand to the small of her back as he escorted her across the street. If he noticed that she had stiffened the moment he'd touched her, he made no mention of it.

And he didn't notice the person in the silver sedan duck down just before he and Tania passed the car.

Nor did he pay attention when the same vehicle started up immediately after he exited the parking structure.

Chapter 10

On the lookout for any sign of her errant daughter, Magda Pulaski was out the bridal shop door and on the sidewalk like a shot before the vehicle even came to a full stop. Definitely before her daughter had a chance to open the car door and get out.

"Ah, finally," Magda declared, clapping her hands together as if in thanksgiving to God for answering her prayers. "Even Marysia is here and she is *always* late."

Hitching her purse onto her shoulder, Tania was already striding toward the shop.

"Sorry, Mama. I lost track of the time." It was a lie. The traffic had been the problem, but saying so would only prompt Mama to ask where she was coming from and so on. Giving Mama an inch usually had her constructing a condominium.

But Magda was not looking at her daughter. Approaching the car, she leaned over to look into its interior, specifically at the driver.

"Is this why you are not tracking time?" she asked, gesturing at Jesse.

Turning back around, Tania hooked onto her mother's arm. "Let's go in, Mama. It's not nice to keep your friend waiting like this," she urged, trying to tug her mother around toward the shop's entrance.

But Magda continued looking into the car. Directly at the lone occupant. "Why you are not getting out?" she asked Jesse.

Tania came to Jesse's defense. "This is a no parking zone," she said, pointing to the sign several feet away.

Magda seemed unimpressed by the information. "It is not parking if he is standing near the car," she argued with the conviction of someone married to a former member of the police force. "Come out," she urged Jesse. "I would like to see you."

"Ma-ma." Tania's voice vibrated with warning. She slanted a quick glance toward Jesse. "You don't have to listen—"

But Jesse was already getting out of his car. As he rounded the front of the vehicle, he extended his hand to the petite, dark-haired woman who was obviously Tania's mother.

"Hello, I'm Jesse Steele."

Magda nodded, slipping her small hand in his. It was obvious that she was pleased the young man had obeyed. She made no effort to hide the fact that he was being scrutinized, dissected and measured by those sharp hazel eyes.

"The hero. Yes, I have read about you," Magda told

him, removing her hand after a beat. "You look better in your skin."

Amused, Jesse grinned. "I'm hardly ever without it."

Tania stifled an exasperated sigh. "She means in person. You look better in person," Tania explained. "She gets her idioms confused."

"You do not have to talk for me," Magda told her, not bothering to turn her head to look at her daughter. She was too busy still assessing the young man who had driven Tania here. "He is understanding what I mean."

Tania rolled her eyes. "Nobody could talk for you, Mama." Again she tugged on her mother's arm, but for a small woman, Magda Pulaski could exude a great deal of strength when she wanted to. Her mother remained exactly where she was. Tania let her hand drop, but insisted, "They're waiting, Mama, remember?"

Magda waved her hand, every iota of her attention focused entirely on the tall, blond-haired, *handsome* man before her. She had questions.

"They were waiting before, they can be waiting a few more minutes." Her eyes pinned him. "You are seeing my daughter?"

"As much as I can," Jesse replied, his amusement growing. He slanted a quick glance in Tania's direction and saw that she was less than happy with her mother's version of the inquisition. "If she lets me."

Nodding, Magda told him confidently, "She will let you." Only then did she turn toward her daughter. "All right, Tatania, say goodbye to him."

Tania shook her head. She should have insisted on taking the bus and spared both of them from witnessing her mother's reenactment of a benevolent dictator.

"Goodbye," she said to Jesse, her teeth only slightly clenched.

Magda frowned. "Not like that. Like a woman says goodbye to a man she is going out with. I will wait in the store." She glanced toward Jesse. "I will not look," she informed with solemnity. Before leaving, she inclined her head toward Jesse. "It is nice to meet you."

Then, turning smartly on her heel, she walked back into the bridal shop. Visible through the large bay window, Magda came to a halt in the center and crossed her arms before her, her back deliberately to the street.

There were no words for this, Tania thought, but she tried. "I'm sorry about that."

"Why? Your mother obviously cares about you. It's nice having people care about you," he added with feeling.

He had a point, of course, but there were times she could have done with a little less "caring."

Tania glanced over her shoulder. She'd thought as much.

"She's watching," she told Jesse.

Jesse looked again at the figure in the bay window. Was he missing something? "Her back is to the window," he pointed out.

Her mother, the illusionist. "The shop has mirrors everywhere," she told him. "Her back might be to the window, but her eyes are fixed on the mirror in the corner. Gives her a perfect view."

Tania saw his mouth curve. A wicked gleam flared in his eyes. "Then let's not disappoint her."

Before she could demur, Tania found herself not just in his arms, but dipped back as if the last note of a passionate tango had just resounded. She was at a forty-five-degree angle.

Her eyes went wide. "What are you doing?"

His grin grew. "Giving your mother what she wants."

And then, there was no more time or space for questions. It was impossible to talk when his lips were sealed to hers. Just like that, her breath deserted her, while the rest of her swiftly turned to jelly. Mama, the bridal shop, the sidewalk, everything, just disappeared.

And just as her head began to spin out of control, Jesse drew his lips away from hers and straightened. His arm was still hooked about the small of her back, for which she was very grateful. Otherwise, she was certain that she would establish a close relationship with the sidewalk below.

Trying hard to breathe, Tania murmured, "Well, that should make her happy."

"She's not the only one," Jesse told her. His expression looked so serious, she wasn't sure if he was pulling her leg or not. "Doctor, you pack quite a punch."

So do you, Jesse.

But it was better for everyone if she kept that thought to herself.

"I better go," she said.

Jesse nodded. He would probably wind up burning the midnight oil—even if every second thought wasn't about her. And if it was, well, then, he knew he might as well prepare himself for an all-nighter.

"Me, too. There are blueprints on the desk at my apartment, waiting for me to make them magical." Damn, but he wanted to kiss her again. And again and again. "I'll see you soon."

She said nothing, merely nodded.

It was hard getting back his bearings. Making his legs function again. Initially he'd kissed Tania for fun, to give her mother a show. But then, once he'd started, he'd wound up giving himself something, as well. At the very least, a great deal to think about.

The only thing he knew for sure right now was that somehow, some way, they were going to make love. There was far too much going on between them for him to ignore or turn his back on out of some sort of half-baked attempt at self-preservation. Tania wasn't Ellen, nor was she like any other woman he'd ever known.

Tania was in a class by herself.

And while she kept putting up obstacles between them, he was certain that Tania felt this pull, this electricity for lack of a better word, between them, too.

He could taste it on her lips, feel it in his soul.

Jesse rounded the front of his car again and got in behind the steering wheel. He had to find a way to make that look of wariness disappear from her eyes.

"So, he knows how to kiss," Mama said with more than a smattering of satisfaction the second Tania entered the shop.

Thinking that discretion was the better part of valor, Tania said nothing.

Over in the corner, wearing one of the wedding gowns and pretending to look at herself from all angles, Natalya couldn't resist saying, "I could have told you that, Mama."

Magda turned and glanced at her second-born sharply. Her pleased look melted away faster than an ice cube in the oven. "Why? You have been kissing him, too?"

"No, Mama," Natalya answered patiently, "I love Mike, remember? But I did see Jesse kissing Tania at the front door of our apartment."

Magda exhaled a deep, no longer troubled breath. Her face softened as she took Tania's hands in hers. "Maybe you would like to look at some of the wedding dresses, too, while you are being here."

"No," Tania told her mother firmly. "No wedding-dress looking. I'm a bridesmaid. I need to find a brides-maid dress. Two," she added as Kady came out from one of the rear dressing rooms wearing a particularly beautiful wedding gown. "Unless you're serious about a double wedding," she said to the two brides. "In which case, Sasha, Marysia and I will need only one."

"Sorry, two," Natalya told her, slowly giving herself the once-over again. "Otherwise, it'll turn into a competition." She turned toward Kady and fluttered her lashes. "And we all know that I'll be the more beautiful bride."

"Ha," Kady countered. "In your dreams, Nat, in your dreams."

Tania knew what her sisters were doing, bless them. They were creating a diversion so that Mama's attention would be directed toward them and not her. Mama would no doubt remember when she had to be the peacemaker when they were all growing up.

"No competition," Magda declared. "There will be two weddings."

"Guess that's that," Kady said, turning around and seeing how well the train moved behind her.

"Yes, Mama," Natalya responded obediently, "whatever you say."

"Two weddings," Magda repeated, then looked at Tania. "For now."

Tania picked up a light blue bridesmaid dress from the nearest rack. This was her cue to duck into a dressing room. She didn't feel up to taking on her mother right now.

"Dr. Pulaski, do you have a minute?" The question, directed to Tania, came from the attractive candy striper. She moved around the desk at the nurses' station, coming into the small, glass-walled alcove that comprised the main station in the E.R.

As happened every so often, just a little more frequently than a blue moon, there was a lull in patient traffic. Tania was hoping to use it to catch up on some of the files she'd left in less than stellar condition. Dr. Howell had been breathing down her neck to rectify her omission.

Even though she knew it was necessary, Tania hated this part of doctoring, hated having to sit and carefully make sense out of her own notes so that anyone could pick up the file and go forward from there. She regarded it much the way she had homework while in school— a necessary evil.

Happy to grasp any excuse, Tania looked up. The woman seemed familiar to her, but for the life of her, Tania couldn't place her.

"That all depends on what side of the paperwork you're on." An excellent surgeon and teacher, Dr. Howell was a stickler for crossing t's and dotting i's and her t's and i's were way overdue. Still, she argued silently, if someone needed medical attention, that came first.

"Why?" Tania glanced past the volunteer down the corridor. "Is there a patient?"

A sheepish expression came over the volunteer's heart-shaped face. "Kind of."

Tania closed the file she'd been working on and rose to her feet. "Where?"

"Here." The candy striper spread her hands to either side of her. Embarrassment colored her neck and cheeks. "Me."

At first glance, there appeared to be nothing wrong with the woman. Her color was good, she wasn't standing in a manner that indicated pain. But then, she could just have been a trooper.

"What's wrong?" Tania asked gamely.

The woman pressed her lips together, as if she loathed to take up a doctor's time. After a moment she said, "It's my back, Doctor—they told me that you're going to be a spinal surgeon," she added quickly.

Tania responded with a small, self-deprecating smile. "In about a hundred years." And some days, it actually felt as if her goal was that far away. Her comment, she noted, seemed to make the woman hesitate. "What about your back?" Tania coaxed.

Relaxing a little, the volunteer placed her hand to the small of her back, as if that helped her manage the pain. "It's been giving me a lot of trouble lately. I think I might have pulled something the other week," she confessed. Lowering her voice so as not to be overheard, she added, "They had me restocking the supply closet and some of the boxes were pretty heavy. I felt a strong twinge on my back when I put one of the boxes up on a high shelf—"

Tania frowned. "You should have asked one of the men to do it."

The volunteer nodded. "I know."

"Why didn't you?" Tania asked.

The question was met with a hapless shrug. "Pride, I guess." She sighed. "Not a very good excuse, I know, but I hate bothering people."

"Okay, you're forgiven," Tania told her. She looked back at the board. Several rooms were empty. "Trauma room three is free. Let's go have a look at that back."

The volunteer smiled broadly. "I appreciate this, Doctor." She stopped, as if realizing she had omitted something. "I'm Carol, by the way."

"Well, Carol-by-the-way—" Tania led the way to the trauma room "—let's see if we can do anything to make you feel better."

"It's all up to you," Carol said as she walked into the room.

That was an odd way to put it, Tania thought. "Why don't you get up on the exam table?" she suggested, crossing to the cabinet.

Opening the top set of doors, Tania took out the glove dispenser. Carol watched her every move. Probably afraid, Tania thought as she slipped on the gloves.

"I was hoping to catch you before you went out to lunch," Carol confided.

"No lunch plans today," Tania told her, approaching the table. "I need you to turn over on your stomach so I can examine your spine."

Carol did as told. "You mean, you're not going out with that guy for lunch?"

Watching Carol shift to her stomach, Tania frowned. "What guy?"

Carol's voice was partially muffled as her cheek was

pressed against the pillow on the table. Her answer came in bits and pieces. "The one who was in the paper. He stopped a robbery. Jason something."

"Jesse," Tania corrected.

"Right, Jesse." Carol raised her head slightly, trying to look at her. "You're not seeing him anymore?"

Tania carefully kneaded her fingers along Carol's spine. "I was never really seeing him."

"Huh." Carol lowered her head again. "I guess I was mistaken. I thought I saw you kissing him the other day. Outside the E.R. doors."

That was where she knew her from, Tania realized. She'd bumped into the woman on her way back into the E.R. that day. "I'm not sure what any of this really has to do with your back pain, Carol."

"Nothing," the young woman said quickly, retreating like a rabbit that had spotted a coyote. "I was just making conversation. I'm sorry, I shouldn't be asking personal questions like that."

She sounded so contrite, Tania felt guilty for being so frosty. "That's okay, I guess I'm a little touchy."

Carol tried to turn her head again. Tania gently pushed her back down. "How come?" And then Carol laughed, the sound rumbling against the exam table. "There I go again, asking more personal questions. My mother always said I was a chatterbox, always talking when I should be listening."

Tania made no comment. Instead she continued to work her fingers up and down the woman's spine. Nothing felt out of the ordinary and Carol had not reacted to her touch.

"Any of this hurt?" she finally asked.

As if on cue, or maybe by coincidence, Carol stiffened, sucking in her breath.

"There," she murmured breathlessly. "Right there. It feels like needles and pins are being pushed into the small of my back."

"You can sit up now," Tania told her. Standing back, Tania stripped off the gloves. She hadn't really needed them this time.

"What's the verdict?" Carol asked, seeming a little like a deer in the headlights.

"It's probably just a strain, but just to be sure, we'll need to take an X-ray. If that doesn't show anything—and a good deal of the time, it doesn't—we might need to take an MRI."

Carol looked intimidated. "An MRI? That's expensive, right?"

Some of them, depending on the number of views done, cost more than two thousand dollars. "Sadly, yes."

Carol shook her head. "I can't afford that," she confessed. She looked embarrassed when she said, "I don't have any health insurance."

Tania figured as much. The woman was a volunteer here, not an employee. If she worked anywhere else, that company might not offer any health insurance, either. "Let me worry about that. For the time being, let's get to the bottom of this pain of yours."

Carol looked hesitant. "I wouldn't want to do anything to get you fired."

"I won't get fired," Tania assured her. Taking the prescription pad out of her pocket, she wrote down a few words on the top sheet, instructions for the radiology department. "Take this to X-ray." Tearing the page off, she held it out to Carol. "You know where that is, right?"

Carol nodded, accepting the paper before getting off the table. "They gave the volunteers a tour of the hospital the first day."

"All right then. Tell them to send the X-rays to me when they're ready. If we don't find anything, then we'll tackle the MRI."

Carol had already crossed to the door. "You're one of a kind, Dr. Pulaski."

Tania smiled to herself. "Actually, I'm one of five," she said under her breath.

Walking out behind Carol, she watched the young woman go down the hall. Either the volunteer was a fledgling hypochondriac, or she was a very stoic soldier because, for someone who said she had back trouble, Carol was moving rather well.

Chapter 11

It seemed to Tania that the candy striper had no sooner turned the corner than the E.R. suddenly came alive again. The back doors sprang open, admitting several sets of paramedics.

Patients poured in, including four people involved in a car accident, each brought in by a separate ambulance. Caught up in the fast pace, Tania lost track of time. And of the candy striper.

It was only at the end of her shift, as she hurriedly went through her files for the day, anticipating the evening ahead of her, that Tania realized that Carol's X-rays had never reached her. They were missing.

And so was Carol.

Guilt and confusion came over her as Tania took a quick peek into the room where she'd initially examined Carol. As she'd suspected, the volunteer wasn't there.

In her place was a rather battered-looking skateboarder, looking none too happy about cooling his heels in the E.R. He had a broken wrist, which was being attended to by Ronald Morris, another one of the fourth-year residents on duty.

In the middle of applying a cast to the grumbling skateboarder's injured wrist, the doctor glanced over in her direction. "Can I help you with something, Dr. Pulaski?"

"Do you know what happened to the patient who was in here a while back?" Tania asked, trying vainly to pinpoint a time.

"They got better?" the doctor suggested whimsically.

"Maybe," Tania murmured, wondering if that was what actually happened. Had Carol felt better and decided not to have the X-rays done?

Tania withdrew from the room. Turning, she noted the head nurse heading toward the central station. She hurried after the woman. "Hey, Shelly, did you see Carol?"

The woman stopped and frowned. "Carol?"

According to Sasha, Shelly had been with the hospital forever and, in her opinion, the woman made it a point to know everyone on staff. "The candy striper." There was no sign of recognition on the older woman's face. "She was complaining about a bad back, so I sent her for X-rays. She was supposed to be in trauma room three."

Habit had Shelly glancing up at the patient board. "You've got a broken wrist in there now. Dr. Morris is treating him."

Tania looked at her watch. It was getting late. She needed to be on her way, but sense of order made her hate leaving things up in the air. "Yes, I know. I was just wondering what happened to Carol."

Shelly lifted her wide shoulders, letting them fall carelessly. "Maybe she changed her mind. Felt better. Happens." And then she looked at Tania over the top of her glasses. "Isn't your shift over, Doctor?"

"Yes, but—"

Shelly's expression told her she wasn't about to be swayed from her position. The chief attending might be at the head of the E.R., but everyone knew that it was Shelly who kept everything running smoothly.

"Go home, Doctor." Tania looked around the area, hoping to spot the missing volunteer. No such luck. Shelly moved her full figure in front of her. "I know it'll be tough but we'll soldier on without you." And then her voice softened. "You're not going to be any good to us if you don't start getting some rest."

Tania felt the corners of her mouth curving. "Since when did you become a doctor?"

Shelly appeared completely unfazed by the question. "I pick things up. Now go." The nurse waved her off to the rear doors.

Tania thought of the play she was seeing tonight. And the man taking her. One stray thought about Jesse and she could feel her anticipation grow. "Actually, I do have somewhere to be."

The woman nodded, turning her attention to the files that were on the desk. "As long as it's not here, that's all I care about."

"It's not," Tania assured her, already backing away, on the path to the lockers. "I'm seeing *Colors of the Rainbow* tonight."

Shelly spared her one long, envious glance. "Lucky dog."

The comment surprised Tania. "I didn't take you for a musical lover."

"I'll have to sing my rendition of *The Impossible Dream* for you someday," Shelly called after her, then chuckled.

It seemed rather appropriate to be seeing this particular play, Tania thought as she boarded the bus on the next corner some ten minutes later. The title actually reflected the way she felt. As if there were a rainbow just beginning inside of her, its collection of colors ready to shoot out of her at a second's notice.

If she were honest with herself, this happiness terrified her. She was afraid to feel this way.

Common sense told her to back away, to cancel tonight and any other "tonights" that might be in the offing. Because not to cancel was to become further involved and becoming further involved would only lead to disaster.

But a stubborn will to soar, to enjoy life, refused to let her cancel or retreat. Refused because there was supposed to be more to life than just going through the motions.

Pros and cons battled it out within her, even as she doggedly continued to move forward.

By the time Tania got off the bus and ran into her building, she had less than twenty minutes to get ready. The elevator seemed to take forever, even though she was the only one on it.

Dashing through the front door of her apartment, she locked it behind her and all but flew to her room.

This time, there was no indecisive hunting through her wardrobe. She knew exactly what she was wearing, a simple black dress that subtly adhered to her figure. That and matching heels. She'd had the foresight to pick it out last night just in case she was running late—which she usually was lately.

When the doorbell rang, she'd just barely finished putting on her makeup. She glanced at her watch. He was five minutes early. The man kept her on her toes.

"Coming," she called out, pausing to step into her shoes. Grabbing the string of pearls she wanted to wear, she flew to the front door, hoping she didn't look as rushed as she felt.

When she got to the door, Tania took a deep breath to center herself, then turned the doorknob to open it. She was still holding on to the necklace.

Jesse was standing on her doorstep, looking better than a man had a living right to.

She tried not to notice that her heart didn't so much skip a beat as jump up in her chest. Either she'd suddenly developed a case of atrial fibrillation, Tania thought, or something was definitely happening here. Something that could have more far-reaching consequences than the condition she'd just diagnosed and discarded.

"You look beautiful," Jesse told her.

So do you, she thought.

Out loud, she said, "Yeah, yeah, I bet you say that to everyone." Tania turned her back to him and held out the pearls while lifting her hair away from her neck. "Could you help me put this on?"

He frowned slightly, taking the pearls from her. He didn't want to help her put on her necklace. He wanted to press his lips against the smooth expanse of skin she'd exposed to him.

Jesse took a breath, reining in his thoughts. "I'm pretty much all thumbs," he confessed. It took him more than one try to hook the clasp. Relieved, he backed away before he wound up giving in to temptation. "Okay," he told her. "Done."

She turned around to face him again and he had this overwhelming desire to kiss her. He banked it down. He'd never been one to allow himself to be governed by impulses.

"And as for saying that to everyone," he commented drily as she grabbed her purse, "I'm pretty sure that this is the first time I'm saying it today." Jesse glanced around just as they were about to leave. "Where's the rest of your team tonight?"

"Elsewhere," she answered simply, fishing out the key to the apartment. "Why, you miss getting the third degree?"

He laughed, shaking his head as Tania locked the door behind them, then slipped her key into her clutch purse. "No, but I was getting used to it. Besides, they were just proving that they cared about you," he told her. "Nice having someone care about you."

"In small doses," she allowed.

He had the distinct feeling that the remark was somehow meant for him.

"Are you aware that you're humming the opening number?" he asked Tania nearly four hours later as she hunted for the key to her apartment door. She'd been humming off and on ever since they'd left the theater and the melodic sound, as well as her pure enjoyment of the play, made him smile. Her eyes were shining. He couldn't recall ever being with a woman whose eyes reflected her inner joy.

Tania stopped humming, but she wasn't embarrassed. It had been a wonderful show, a wonderful evening all around, and right at this moment, she felt incredibly content and happy.

Looking up from her purse, she nodded. "I know. The song was wonderful. The whole play was wonderful." Her eyes smiled at him as her fingers located her keys. "*Everything* was wonderful."

Including the time she'd shared with him. They'd gone to a five-star restaurant not too far from the theater. Then, because his car was parked in a structure, they decided to leave it there and walk to the theater. It was a warm, sultry night and they continued their conversation from the restaurant. There'd been no awkward pauses, no hunting for something to say. She discovered that they liked the same movies, the same authors, the same baseball team.

For the life of her, Tania couldn't remember when she'd enjoyed herself so much.

"No argument from me," Jesse assured her softly.

She could almost feel his eyes caressing her face. Could feel her heart start hammering even before his lips touched hers.

Tania threaded her arms around his neck and gave herself up to the moment, silently arguing that since it was for the moment, it was all right.

The keys slipped from her lax fingers as she lost herself in the kiss. But just as it felt as if it was going to continuing building, Jesse drew back.

"You dropped your keys," he told her, bending to pick them up for her.

"I guess my fingers went numb." Her eyes danced with

amusement. Taking the keys from him, she inserted one in the keyhole. And discovered that the door was unlocked. "That's weird," she murmured under her breath.

"What is?"

She pushed the door open slowly. "The door wasn't locked."

"Maybe one of your sisters came home and forgot to lock it." He'd done it himself once or twice when his mind was on other things.

But Tania shook her head. She was still standing on the threshold, peering in. He saw the uneasy look in her eyes. "My father was on the police force for twenty-seven years. He drummed that into our heads—always lock your door behind you, coming and going, even if you're only home for five minutes. It's just something we do."

"Maybe I'd better look around for you," he suggested.

Independence warred with common sense. Common sense won. "Sure."

Tania banked down the surge of nervousness that threatened to overwhelm her. She was grateful to him for volunteering rather than waiting to be asked. But she didn't want him to think she was one of those women who needed to check her closets and look under her bed before she went to sleep each night.

Still, the first thing that popped into her head was that somehow, after all this time had passed, Jeff had broken in.

That Jeff was waiting for her.

C'mon, Tania. Stop being an idiot. She forced a smile to her lips. "Miss being the hero?"

Jesse made his way through the living room. "I'm not a hero yet," he told her. "That's only if there's a bad guy hiding in one of your closets and I get to engage him in hand-to-hand combat." He noticed how quiet it was. If someone else was home, he was fairly certain that by now, they'd be out to investigate. "Your sisters still aren't home?"

"Apparently not," she murmured. Then, in an audible voice, said, "Doctors keep erratic hours."

Jesse slanted a smile in her direction. "I'm beginning to learn that. Why don't you stay by the door while I check the rest of the apartment out?" he suggested.

"The hell I will," was her answer.

She wasn't a shrinking violet. He had to admit he liked that about her. "Okay, then stay behind me, just in case."

Her breath caught in her throat even as she tried to brazen it out. "Why? Do you think that someone's still here?"

"Probably not. But it doesn't hurt to be cautious. I had a friend who walked in on a burglar once. Burglar was so scared, he almost trampled my friend trying to get out." Jesse looked at her meaningfully. "But some burglars *aren't* afraid."

"I know," she said quietly.

With Tania half a breath behind him, Jesse made his way from room to room. There was no one else in the apartment. When they walked into the last room, the kitchen, Jesse saw two notes posted on the refrigerator door, held in place by magnets, one shaped like a stethoscope, the other like a miniature Empire State Building.

Moving ahead of him, Tania read first one note, then the other. Natalya's note said she was at their parents' in Queens and would probably spend the night there, while Kady's note, which appeared to have been left first, said she was spending quality time with her fiancé.

"Quality time?" Jesse echoed. He'd only heard the term applied to parents and children.

Tania grinned. "That's code for spending the night," she told him. She saw his quizzical look and beat him to the obvious question. "We use code in case one of our parents stops by and sees the note."

"Your parents don't approve of Kady's fiancé?" He'd only met her briefly, but Magda Pulaski didn't strike him as a woman who would hold her tongue if she disapproved of something or someone.

Tania was quick to correct the misimpression. "Oh, no, they love him." She led the way back to the living room. "He saved Kady's life."

A knowing smile curved his mouth. "Then it's your sister sleeping with him before they're married that's the problem?" he guessed.

It sounded so unforgiving when he said it and her parents were warm, caring people with huge hearts.

"My parents aren't prudes." She wanted him to know that. The next moment she asked herself why that was important. "They just don't want it stuck in their faces."

He nodded. Sexuality was a difficult thing for one generation to accept about another—and it worked both ways, he thought. He never wanted to think about the possibility of his mother dating after his father was killed.

Jesse glanced toward the door. He knew it was time to leave, even if he didn't want to.

"Well, I guess it looks like one of your sisters did forget to close the door when she left. There's no one here but us," he added needlessly, looking down into her face. "I guess I'd better get going."

Tania caught the bottom of her lip between her teeth, debating. In a minute she'd be home free. Despite that, she heard herself saying, "Since you're already inside, would you like to stay awhile? I could make some coffee—or maybe you'd rather have a drink?" As she asked, she made her way over to the small liquor cabinet against the far wall.

"Sounds good," he acknowledged, right behind her. He glanced into the cabinet as she opened the double doors. "What do you have?"

Tania stepped back and turned around to give him a better view. Which was her mistake. Her body brushed against his. Instantly her pulse quickened. Breath caught in her throat, she turned her face up to his.

Jesse didn't need more of an invitation. Ever so lightly, he framed her face with his hands and brought his mouth down to hers again.

Something exploded inside of her. Something fierce and overpowering.

Her breath came in quick snatches as her head began to spin. One thought throbbed in her brain. Quickly, this had to be done quickly.

Before she could think.

Before she could remember.

Her mouth still sealed to his, Tania urgently pushed his jacket from his shoulders, tugging the sleeves down his arms. She needed to hurry, to go as fast as she could in order to outrace instincts bent on stopping her. On protecting her from the very thing she found herself craving and wanting.

Without any warning, Jesse felt as if he suddenly had a whirlwind in his arms. His blood heated and it was all he could do not to follow her lead, not to drag her dress from her body. But if he did, if he kept pace with Tania, then their lovemaking would be over with almost before it began. It wasn't his way and even if it were, he sensed that there was far too much going on here for him to race to the finish line like that.

So when her eager fingers began to fumble with the clasp on his belt, Jesse caught them in both his hands, stilling them even though desire all but slammed into him with the force of a Mack truck.

"Hey, hey, hey," he chided softly. Still holding her hands in one of his, he caressed her cheek with the other. There was something in her eyes that he couldn't place. Fear? "What's your hurry, Tania? Got a plane to catch?"

Her hands trembled within his. "No," she breathed.

Please, please, please, don't stop me, don't let me think. Please don't let me remember.

Jesse brought his lips down to the side of her neck, skimming the delicate skin there. Excitement soared through his veins.

"Then let's take this nice and slow," he whispered coaxingly. Taking her by the hand, he asked, "Which was your room?"

"The second one," she answered breathlessly. She moved ahead of him, striding down the hall as if the devil was after her.

Because, in a way, he was.

The second she was inside her room, Tania pushed the door closed with the flat of her hand. "All right," she managed to get out.

Whether it was a question or a statement, he didn't know. He was only aware that she'd all but glued herself to him. The rush was incredible and he nearly lost his bearings right there. It took superhuman control not to give in to the urges that threatened to tear him apart.

They tumbled onto the bed, clothes leaving their bodies in unsyncopated rhythm until they were both nude, pressed against one another.

Tania felt as if she was on fire. On fire and at the same time, in danger of being doused by a huge bucket of ice. Because the memory of *that* night was never that far out of reach. It was always ready to claim her.

Jesse kissed her over and over again, but it was already too late. Too late because fear had reared its head, freezing her body. She struggled to keep it at bay, to push the fear back so that she could lose herself in what was happening.

She won small victories, but the war was, for the most part, lost. Her body ceased heating as his touch, so gentle, brought back memories of another touch, far less gentle. A touch that was hard, grasping. Possessive.

It wasn't fair to him, Tania thought, fighting back tears. Not fair to Jesse. Not fair to her to feel like this, to be locked away from what she felt certain, in her heart, was wondrously pleasurable and good.

She did her best to seem eager, to keep up the illusion that they were on the same wavelength, all the while hoping against hope to somehow unlock the door to the cell that kept her a prisoner. The cell that kept her from him.

But in the end, as he murmured her name against her ear and entered her, Tania could only congratulate herself for putting on a believable act. She tried to mimic his movements, to make him think that they came to the crest together when all she wanted was to shrink back, to have it done with.

When his weight suddenly sank against her, she knew it was over.

The sadness that seized her heart was almost excruciating.

Pivoting on his elbows, Jesse drew his head back and looked down at her. She'd turned her head away from him, but he thought he saw a tear in the corner of her eye.

So he wasn't wrong in what he'd felt, Jesse thought, far from happy about being right. He withdrew and lay down beside her. He had no idea what to make of what had just happened here. Because it had never happened to him before.

Taking a breath, he slipped his arm around Tania and drew her closer to him. He felt Tania stiffen. Could almost feel her forcing herself to relax. This wasn't right.

With the tips of his fingers, he moved her hair away from her cheek. "Where were you?" he asked quietly.

Tania forced a smile to her lips. Reaching around for the comforter, she drew it up over herself to cover her nakedness. "I'm not that thin. I was right here." The solemn expression on his face made her nervous.

"Your body was," he agreed.

Holding on to the comforter tightly, she raised herself up to look at him. "Are you trying to tell me you were disappointed?"

"No—and yes," he told her honestly. Tania began to get up and he blocked her move. "We just made love, but you weren't there. You were literally MIA—missing in action." Jesse gently tapped her temple. Her eyes were huge, he thought. Was she afraid of him? He didn't understand. "Where were you?" he repeated.

Her breath was shaky as she released it. "I'm sorry if it wasn't good for you—"

"I didn't say that," he interrupted patiently. "If anything, maybe it wasn't good for you." She seemed surprised at his willingness to take the blame. "Because if it had been, you would have been there, just as wrapped up in it, as grateful to be part of it, as I was. But you weren't."

Tania felt torn and tortured. He was asking the right questions, the questions she didn't want to face, didn't want to answer. He deserved better. He deserved more than she could give him.

Fighting tears, she touched his face. "Don't get involved with me, Jesse."

The laugh that came from his lips had no humor to it. "I think it's too late for that warning. The question is, why won't you get involved with me?" He took her hand in his. "Is it something I've done?"

She closed her eyes, lost. Wishing she hadn't let it get this far. "Oh no, no, it's not you. Well, it is, but it's not. It is because you're on the unfortunate receiving end of this. It's not because you are damn near perfect."

That made absolutely no sense to him, but he played along. "Is that a flaw?" he asked. "Because if it is, I can be imperfect," he offered. "I could trip you before we make love again."

She stared at him, stunned. "You want to make love again?"

How could she even ask? "I want to make love with you for as many days as there are in a month. Every month."

This after she'd gone cold, Tania thought. How could anyone be this good? And how could she allow herself to jeopardize this? How could she break out of her prison? "Wow."

"That wasn't quite the answer that I expected—I was hoping for a 'me, too,'" he told her with a grin. "But I can work with 'wow.'"

"Why would you want to?" she asked. "Why would you want to make love with me again? Why would you want to stay?"

"Because if I do, then maybe you'll learn to trust me enough to let me in—or at least give me the name of the guy who did this to you so I could kill him."

His voice was so mild, uttering the words, she laughed despite herself. It had a sad, hollow sound. "You'd have to forfeit your Good Samaritan standing."

"I don't care," he told her, deadly serious. "It would be worth it."

Tania watched him for a long moment. He wasn't just mouthing what he thought she needed to hear. Jesse was serious.

She began to cry.

Chapter 12

Jesse never felt so helpless as when faced with a woman's tears. He vividly remembered the moment when his mother found out that his father hadn't survived the gunshot wound he'd sustained during the robbery of their grocery store. He'd given her the news and had been at a complete loss when she'd burst into tears.

At the time, no words could afford her any comfort. Little had changed over the years. No real words of comfort came to him now in the face of Tania's silent tears. All he could do was take her into his arms and hold her, give her the silent comfort of his arms and his presence.

Jesse let a few moments go by before he asked, "Do you want to tell me about it?"

Jesse's question scraped the depths of her soul. She didn't want to talk about it, hadn't said a word about the incident in years. Not since the assistant D.A. had told her that Jeff and his defense counsel were accepting a plea bargain. Back then, countless months after the rape, she'd been forced to sit in the closed courtroom, listening to Jeff own up to what he'd done. Listening to Jeff apologize and ask forgiveness for the unforgivable.

It had all felt so surreal then. She'd been the good little victim, she'd brought her rapist up on charges so that he wouldn't do to someone else what he'd done to her. And then, after it was over and the judge and the two opposing lawyers went back to their lives, she'd been left to deal with the black hole that Jeff's attack had created inside of her.

Her way of dealing with it was to try to fill the hole up any way she could, with work and by searching for someone who would make her forget, who could make her finally move on. But all she'd ever managed to do was find men who, by the very act of lovemaking, caused her to remember. And to regret.

Tania took in a long, ragged breath. Jesse was right. This had to come out. If nothing else, she owed him that. Owed herself that.

"I was seventeen years old, invincible, and as trusting as a puppy. And Jeff was the handsomest thing I'd ever seen. A college freshman. And my friend. Or so I thought." Tania pressed her lips together to keep back the sob that erupted in her throat.

"Take your time," Jesse said softly, his arms tightening ever so slightly around her. Close enough to protect, but not tight enough to cause her to feel trapped.

Tania shrugged helplessly, her cheek pressed against his chest, her eyes looking into the past. "It's the usual story. We were at a party, he had too much to drink. I drove him to his dorm. It was the beginning of spring break and it seemed like everyone was gone." How many times had she gone over this in her mind? If only she'd left him at the entrance of the building, things would have been different. *She* would have been different. If only… "So I helped him up to his room and suddenly, once we were inside, it somehow turned into a wrestling match."

She paused again. When she spoke, her voice was shaky. It cracked several times. "I always thought that, in a situation like that, I'd know what to do, how to get away. My father taught all of us self-defense, drilled us on how to take care of ourselves." Her mouth dry, she ran her tongue along her lips, trying to moisten them. Each word she uttered seemed to stick to the roof of her mouth. "I honestly thought I could talk Jeff out of it. I thought I could handle him—until I couldn't."

Tania closed her eyes, tears seeping through her lashes. Jesse could feel them against his chest as they slid down her cheek. He remained quiet, letting her tell him at her own pace.

"And then he was like somebody else, somebody I didn't know," she said heavily. "Had never known. He raped me and fell asleep. Like it was nothing," Tania whispered, her voice cracking again.

Jesse felt anger surging within him, explosive anger. It took effort to keep it from taking over. But there was no one in the room except for the two of them. No one to lash out at, to make pay for the crime committed against this woman.

He stroked her hair, silently telling her she could lean on him. "Did you tell anyone?"

She sat up then and wrapped her arms around her knees, drawing them into herself. The comforter pooled around her.

"I didn't have to. My father was waiting up. He took one look at me when I came in through the door and he knew. He *knew.* They were very good to me, my parents," she murmured. The tears continued to flow down her cheeks, mingling with the ends of her hair. "But my father wouldn't let me bury it. He told me that the rape would always haunt me until I brought Jeff to justice." She exhaled loudly. "So I did, and for the most part, my father was right." A touch of irony entered her voice. "They all think I'm okay, my sisters, my parents. And I am. Usually. Except when I freeze up inside." She turned her head, looking at him over her shoulder. "So you see, Jesse, it's really not you, it's me."

"No," he answered very gently, "it's him. That worthless piece of trash who raped you, *he's* keeping you from moving on. He robbed you of your trust, kept you from enjoying something very basic, very vital." Jesse ran the back of his knuckles gently along her cheek. "Don't let him do that to you."

Too late, she thought. She tried to smile and failed dismally. "You're being awfully nice."

"Haven't you heard?" he teased. "Heroes are supposed to take Nice 101 before they're allowed to rescue someone. Can't do a decent rescue without it."

Her smile was marked with sadness. "Is that what you're going to do? Rescue me?"

I'll do anything you want me to. The ease with which the thought came to him surprised Jesse. And it felt right. "Can't think of anyone I'd rather rescue than you."

He was being so good about this that she felt even guiltier. Tania shook her head. "I'm sorry I spoiled this for you."

"The only way you could have spoiled it for me is by not being here in the first place. Then, of course," he added with a teasing smile, "I'd be arrested for breaking and entering because I would have had no business being in your apartment."

Something stirred inside of Tania that she hadn't felt before. Not about someone outside her family. She'd only been on the brink of infatuation once and that had been with Jeff. And then he'd shattered her. Since then she'd never reacted to any male on anything but a physical level.

But this was something different, beyond the basic pull of attraction she'd felt. Something she couldn't— wouldn't—put a name to. At least not yet. Naming it would only jinx it.

She laughed at his protest. "You make me feel... safe," she confessed to Jesse after a beat.

He pretended to be disappointed. "And here I thought I had this bad-boy thing going."

The smile that curved her mouth was far less difficult to summon. And, miraculously, some of the sadness was gone.

Tania cleared her throat. She'd asked men out before, but this was different. Harder.

"If you want to give it another try..." Her voice trailed off.

Jesse cupped her cheek with his palm. "You already know the answer to that," he told her. "But only if you're ready and you want to."

She looked at him incredulously. "Otherwise, you'd wait?"

He nodded. "Otherwise, I'd wait." He brushed his fingertip along her cheek, capturing a precious bit of dampness. "You're crying again."

"Good tears," she told him, trying hard, and unsuccessfully, to stop. "Good tears."

"Good tears, bad tears." Jesse shook his head, mystified. "I don't understand how you can cry when you're happy," he told her honestly. "But I'll take your word for it."

Tilting her chin up, Jesse gently brushed his lips against hers. And then again. And again, each time a little deeper than the last, a little longer than the last.

One arm around her, he moved her closer against him. His free hand delved beneath the comforter and, very slowly, he caressed her, lightly tracing the outline of her hip.

His movements were languid, as if she were a wild mare that had wandered onto his property and he was afraid of spooking her, of driving her away.

Even as the urges multiplied within him, Jesse kept himself in check. Like a man inching his way across a tightrope stretched over the Grand Canyon, where any misstep could be his last, Jesse made love to every part of her. Slowly, one movement building on another.

He took his cues from her, listening to her intake of breath, feeling her heart hammering against his. Ever on the alert for her shrinking back because that would mean that he needed to back off a little before he could move forward.

It was all about her and because he succeeded in

.arousing her, because he heard her moan with pleasure, he experienced triumph upon triumph.

No part of her was left untouched, uncaressed, unkissed, until he felt her movements accelerate, not as if she were in some sort of race to finish quickly, but because she was in the midst of a fever pitch.

Drawing the length of his body over hers, Jesse joined his hands with Tania's, threading his fingers through hers and making them one before the actual physical act reinforced that.

"Are you all right?" he whispered in her ear.

She didn't answer. Instead she moved her legs apart and let him enter. Rather than stiffen the way she had last time, the way she had every time since she'd been attacked, Tania arched her hips, a silent invitation. The heat and desire traveling through her body moved everything else into the background.

This time she actually felt the rhythm overtake her rather than her struggling to mimic the movement of his hips.

And then, for the first time in her life, she let this incredible sensation vibrate through her, making her scramble toward the feeling, wanting more even as she savored its essence. It seemed to her like an explosion that kept on going.

Enthralled, Tania grasped hold of his shoulders, arching higher, seeking to prolong the moment. And then, when it was over, she sank into this soft, welcoming cloud. Her pulse slowly decelerated.

What had just happened here? She felt like such a novice.

Tania opened her eyes and saw him, still pivoted on

his elbows, looking down at her face. There was concern in his eyes.

"Are you all right?" he asked softly.

It took her a minute to find her tongue. Longer to locate her wits. Try as she might, she couldn't even begin to define what she was feeling, other than overwhelmed.

And powerful.

And free.

"So all right that they haven't even invented the word to cover how all right I am," she finally answered, her voice barely audible. She drew in two more deep breaths and then released them. Her odd euphoria was wondrous. "I think I might have just had an out-of-body experience."

Jesse did his best not to laugh. But he did smile. Broadly. Smiled and pressed a kiss to her temple. Getting off her, he moved to the side and tucked his arm around her again, once more drawing her to him. "Then I guess that my work here is done."

She turned her face into his. They were barely inches apart. So close that she could taste his breath. And found herself aroused again. "Is that what you call it? Work?"

"I call it ecstasy, personally," he confessed. And then Jesse kissed her again, softly, tenderly, not like a man who wanted to make love again, but like a man who loved.

She nodded at his response, curling into him. Thrilled beyond words that she wanted to, that she didn't want to bolt and run or hurl herself into an hour-long shower.

"Sounds like a good call to me," she murmured.

She splayed her hand along his chest, sinking further into a web of contentment. Resting her head against his shoulder, Tania was soon asleep.

Jesse lay there beside her, listening to her breathe, so moved by the simple act that he hardly recognized himself. It was a little scary, he mused, feeling all these different sensations.

He felt protective toward this woman. Protective and completely and unnervingly at her mercy.

There was an interpretation for all this and he knew it, but right now, he didn't want to explore what it meant. Tonight, he would bask in the triumph generated by all the walls that had been breached.

Jesse remained with her for a while longer. Her breathing remained steady. No nightmares assaulted her, no sudden fits and starts overtook her. Only sleep.

And then, very slowly, so as not to wake Tania up, Jesse retreated from her. When his arm was clear of her body, he sat up and then got off the bed.

It was late.

He was acutely aware that one or both of her sisters might come home anytime now despite the notes they'd left on the refrigerator. He had a feeling that Tania might not want to explain his presence to them.

To spare Tania the awkwardness, he decided to leave. Moreover, if she awoke to regret having trusted him with her secret, or her body, he didn't want to see all that reflected in her eyes. She had such expressive eyes.

Taking his clothes into her bathroom, Jesse got dressed quickly. And then, very quietly, carrying his shoes in his hand, Jesse left the apartment. He pulled the door closed behind him.

He heard the tumbler click as the lock fell into place.

After pausing at the door to put on his shoes, Jesse walked quickly to the elevator. He passed no one in the corridor, but he had the distinct, uneasy feeling that someone was there.

This was a bad time to be paranoid, he thought. It was all just in his head, he assured himself. Residue from when Ellen had stalked him, nothing more. Even so, he paused by the elevator, listening before he pressed the down button.

There was nothing to hear.

Jesse had walked all the way to the parking structure and was actually sitting in his car, his key in the ignition, about to turn the engine on, when he had a change of heart. Concern about Tania got the better of him.

He'd been thinking of himself when he left.

His unwillingness to see regret on Tania's face had prompted him to go. He hadn't really thought about it in terms of how *she* would feel if she woke up to find him gone. What if she didn't feel relief when she reached out only to find that space beside her empty?

What if the wrong message was sent by his absence from her bed? What if Tania felt abandoned? Or even used?

A lot of one-night stands slipped out in the middle of the night, leaving their partners to face the dawn alone. That wasn't what he wanted her to think. At the very least, he wanted her to know that this was not a one-night stand. Not to him.

What the hell had he been thinking, leaving like that? Jesse upbraided himself.

Exiting the vehicle, he paused only long enough to lock it again. And then he hurried back the long city block to her building.

Getting in the building's front door was no problem.

He rang a series of doorbells until someone's voice finally crackled over the intercom.

"Jake, is that you?" a husky woman's voice asked.

"Yeah," he rasped.

The woman cursed on the other end and, for a second, Jesse thought he would have to go on pressing buttons. But then the harsh sound of the buzzer filled the air. He lost no time pushing the heavy door open.

A great deal of pent-up energy coursed through his veins. It had been roughly about fifteen minutes or so since he'd left. Jesse crossed his fingers and hoped that Tania hadn't woken up in the interval.

Entering the lobby, he glanced at the dial above the closed elevator door. The car was on the fifth floor. Her floor. Too impatient to wait for the elevator car to make its way down to the first floor, Jesse decided to take the stairs instead.

He raced up all five flights and was breathing heavily when he threw open the door that led out onto her floor. He didn't pause to catch his breath. Instead he hurried over to her apartment. Knowing the outcome ahead of time, he tried the door anyway. It was locked, just the way he'd left it.

It wasn't a problem.

He'd had a lot of friends in his youth, not all with savory backgrounds that followed straight and narrow paths. One of his former friends was currently serving five to seven upstate for burglary. The same former friend who had once taught him how to pick any lock "in case of an emergency."

Jesse was determined to let himself in without waking Tania if he could. If possible, he didn't want her to even suspect that he had ever left.

Because it had been a very long time since he'd attempted to pick any lock—sheerly for practice—it took him several attempts and as many minutes to finally conquer the lock. Trying the doorknob, he felt it give beneath his hand. As quietly as possible, he turned the doorknob all the way and opened the door.

The second he walked into the apartment, he smelled it.

Gas.

Chapter 13

Jesse didn't even stop to think, he just reacted. Dashing into the apartment, he began throwing windows open as he made his way to Tania's bedroom.

He found her just the way he'd left her, in bed and sound asleep. The only difference was, when he shook her to wake her up, Tania remained unresponsive. The smell of gas began to get to him but he focused on what he had to do. Get Tania out of there as quickly as he could.

Throwing off the comforter, he wrapped her nude body in a sheet and picked her up. His throat felt scratchy and his head began to spin. Trying to breathe as little as possible, Jesse carried her out of the apartment and into the hall.

He leaned a still-unconscious Tania against the wall right next to the apartment door. As he squatted beside her, at a complete loss as to what to do, his mind raced.

He started rubbing her wrists, hoping that if he got her circulation going, he could make her come around.

He endured several very scary minutes, watching her face as he continued to rub. Just as he was about to call 9-1-1, her eyes fluttered open. She moaned and then began to cough as she put her hand to her head.

He sat back on his heels for a second, looking at her, so relieved he could barely catch his own breath. "Oh, thank God."

Tania stared at him, unseeing and disoriented, her head pounding like the inside of a bowling alley when all the lanes were in play. Taking a deep breath and blinking, she slowly looked around, trying to get her bearings. Trying to focus. Where was she? And then it came to her.

"Jesse, what are we doing out in the hallway?" As bits and pieces became clearer, she looked down at herself. And saw she had the top sheet from her bed wrapped around her like a blue flowing toga. What the hell was going on? "Am I still naked?" she asked him incredulously.

"You're still alive," he corrected. Suddenly feeling light-headed himself, Jesse shifted so that his back was against the wall, too. Leaning, he sank beside her. At the moment, his knees didn't quite feel as if they could support him.

She didn't understand what he was saying. "Why wouldn't I be?" she asked. "And *what* are we doing out here?"

Tania hoped he had some kind of plausible answer for this. Had she been wrong about him, after all? Had she let her barriers down just to allow some kind of weirdo closer to her?

Her nerves began to shift even as something inside her head whispered for her to withhold final judgment.

He wanted to take her into his arms, to hug her and hold her to him and just listen to her breathe. But right now, if he gauged the look in her eyes correctly, that would probably frighten her.

So instead he told her, "There's a gas leak in your apartment."

Holding the sheet to her, bracing one hand against the doorjamb, Tania rose shakily to her feet. He sprang to his, as if ready to catch her if she fell.

"That's not possible," she insisted. "Kady said we just had someone come through the other day, checking to make sure everything was up to code." And then her eyes widened slightly as she remembered. "The building's super even replaced the old gas stove with a new one."

Something just didn't make sense. Had a faulty stove been put in on purpose? Why? By who? He needed to look around. "Stay here," he ordered.

"Naked in the hall?" she demanded. Granted it was the middle of the night and probably no one would pass by, but she wasn't about to stay here to find out. "I don't think so."

But as she started to follow him, Tania suddenly swayed, her light-headedness getting the better of her.

Alert, Jesse moved back and caught her before she could sink to her knees. "Stay put," he told her firmly. Both hands on her shoulders, he pressed her back against the outside wall and then went inside the apartment.

The late evening air came in through all the windows he'd opened and began to cut into the overpowering smell of gas. But he could still smell it.

Walking into the kitchen, Jesse immediately saw that all four burners had been turned on. They were on, but not a single blue flame was visible. He looked at the knobs that ran along the side of the stovetop. Someone had deliberately turned on the gas jets while making sure that the flames had been extinguished.

Why?

"What did you find?"

Jesse swung around to see Tania in the kitchen doorway, looking pale but determined to be there. She held the sheet to her with one hand, while grasping the doorjamb with the other to keep herself steady.

He banked down a surge of anger. What did it take to make the woman stay put? "That you don't take instruction well."

Tania waved her hand at the comment, her attention on the stove. "We already knew that." Her eyes narrowed as she came forward. "Is the stove on?"

"Apparently." Taking a kitchen towel, Jesse held it against his fingers and turned all four jets back to "off" before she could do it herself.

"What are you doing?" she asked.

"Whoever turned the gas jets on probably left their fingerprints."

Whoever. That meant someone had come in and done this on purpose. That wouldn't have been the first thing she would have thought of. Tania's mouth curved slightly.

"You've been watching too much television." She had a more logical explanation. "Kady or Natalya probably just forgot to turn off the stove."

"Like they forgot to lock the door?" he asked pointedly.

Her head jerked up as her thought process leapfrogged. "Do you think something happened to one of them?"

She was agitated, so he spoke calmly, putting his hand on her arm to steady her. "No. And I don't think either one of them left unlit burners on, either. We would have smelled something earlier," he pointed out.

She nodded. That made sense. What didn't make sense was why the burners had been turned on in the first place. And by who?

Tania shook her head. The throbbing was getting worse. "This is just so strange. One weird thing after another," she murmured, more to herself than to him.

But she had his undivided attention. "What do you mean, one weird thing after another? What other weird thing are you talking about?"

She looked at him, debating. He was probably going to think she was a little crazy. Or maybe a lot. "I can't shake this feeling that someone is watching me. And the other day—" She paused, searching for a way to say this without sounding dramatic. "I was nearly hit by a bus."

He stared at her, stunned. Was she putting him on? "What?"

Tania shrugged, as if it was really nothing and she was sorry she'd mentioned it. "I was standing on the corner, waiting for the light to change, and I guess it was too crowded because suddenly it felt like someone pushed me from behind. I started to fall forward and if that guy hadn't grabbed my arm and pulled me back, I would have been road kill."

She was embarrassed by the revelation, he realized. She *wasn't* putting him on, but she was trying to downplay it. "Why didn't you say anything before?" he asked.

An awkwardness descended over her. She struggled against feeling like a victim. The way she'd struggled off and on all these years.

Again she shrugged, looking away. "Didn't see the point. There are eight million people in the city and sometimes two or more try to occupy the same space, especially on a street corner. Accidents are bound to happen."

One was an accident, two or more made for an unnerving pattern. He knew all about denial. He's used it as a tool when he was being stalked.

Jesse glared at the stove. "Maybe too many accidents." He didn't want to ask, but he came to the only logical conclusion he could. "Does this Jeff know where you live these days?"

Tania suddenly felt cold. Trying to bank down the feeling, she ran her hands over her arms. "You think this might be him?"

"I don't know. I'm not the police." He came over to stand beside her and slipped his arm around her shoulders. "I think we should call them."

She shook her head so hard, she nearly became dizzy again. "No. I don't want this getting back to my father. He has connections all over the force. He'll worry." She could see that Jesse wasn't about to back away. She hit on a compromise. "I'll call Sasha's husband. He won't say anything to my father."

She'd mentioned to him that Tony Santini was a homicide detective. Jesse nodded. "As long as you call someone," he told her. "How do you feel?"

Tania raised her chin and forced a smile to her lips. She was *not* going to be the object of pity, especially not his. "Like I have my own private hero."

He didn't reciprocate her smile. "I'm serious, Tania. I couldn't get you to wake up at first." He swept her hair back from her face. "Maybe you should go to the hospital and get checked out."

Tania stepped back and he instinctively knew he wasn't going to get her to listen unless he slung her over his shoulder and carried her to the hospital.

"I'm an E.R. doctor. I can check myself out as easily as any of them," she insisted. "Physician heal thyself and all that stuff."

"This isn't funny, Tania. If I hadn't come back—"

"Come back?" she echoed, surprised. "From where? When I fell asleep, you were right there." And then it suddenly dawned on her. He wasn't wearing a sheet, he had his clothes on. He wouldn't have stopped to get dressed before getting her out of the apartment. "Why are you dressed? When I fell asleep, you were naked."

He had wanted to avoid having her find out the truth, but there was no getting around it now. "I thought maybe one of your sisters might come home unexpectedly and I didn't want you to have to explain what I was doing there."

"I wouldn't have had to explain. They're both doctors. They both have a pretty good handle on the birds and the bees thing." She dropped her sarcastic tone and her voice was low, serious. "So what made you come back?"

There were a lot of ways to couch this, but he gave it to her as honestly as he could. "I realized that if you woke up in an empty bed, you might feel a little abandoned." His eyes met hers. "And I really didn't want that."

She took in a deep, fortifying breath. Her lungs still

ached and her head felt a little fuzzy. But not her heart. That felt just fine. "You didn't?"

"No, I didn't." He wasn't about to be sidetracked. Jesse took out his cell phone. Flipping it open, he placed the phone into her hand. "Now call your brother-in-law."

Tania closed the phone in a fluid movement and handed it back to him. "It's after one in the morning. I'll call him at a more decent hour."

Jesse didn't accept the phone. Instead he pressed it back into her hand. "He's a policeman, he's used to strange hours. Call him," he said firmly. "Or I'll call 9-1-1. Your choice."

She sighed, frowning at the phone. "So much for twisting you around my little finger."

"I wouldn't fit." Jesse nodded at the phone. "Which will it be?"

There was no real choice. "I'll call Tony. Can I at least get dressed?"

He smiled for the first time, his eyes sweeping over her frame. Remembering what she'd looked like, pliant and giving, in his arms. "For the sake of Sasha and Tony's marriage, I'd highly recommend it."

A little more than half an hour later, Tony, Sasha, Mike, who had been called to the scene by Tony, and Natalya arrived almost simultaneously at the apartment. Using Sasha's old key, Tony unlocked the door and came in first.

Jesse and Tania were on their feet instantly, meeting them in the foyer before they'd taken more than one step into the apartment.

Tony had been filled in about the gas leak over the

phone when Tania called him. His concern was evident, even if his expression remained stoic. "Are you all right?" he asked Tania. She nodded. Tony turned toward his wife. "She's all right." There was a strange finality about his voice, as if he had just proven a point. "Now will you go back home?" Without waiting for an answer, he turned toward his sister-in-law's fiancé. "Mike, can you take her—"

Moving forward, Sasha sniffed the air. "I don't smell any gas," she said, interrupting her husband. "No need to rush me out of here, Tony. The baby'll be fine," she assured him, then turned toward Tania. "My question is, are you sure you're all right?"

Tania nodded, feeling bad about having dragged not one but four members of her family out of bed. "This is all getting out of hand," she protested. "It was just a leak, nothing more."

"This wasn't a leak," Jesse insisted. "Leaks don't suddenly stop when you turn a knob on the stove." He looked from one detective to another, realizing that the men probably had no idea who he was. "Hi, I'm Jesse Steele. I'm the one who insisted she call you. Or the police," he tacked on.

"Same thing," Tony said, shaking Jesse's outstretched hand. "Tony Santini."

"Mike DiPalma." Mike took his turn shaking Jesse's hand. "And it's not the same thing," he corrected Tony. "It's better." He looked at his future sister-in-law. "All right, tell us what happened. From the beginning," he qualified.

"I was asleep," she explained, then turned toward Jesse. "You fill them in."

So Jesse did, as quickly and succinctly as he could.

Ending his story, he added that he'd just found out from Tania that she'd been pushed in the path of an oncoming bus and that for the last few weeks, she'd been trying to shake the feeling that she was being watched.

Mike nodded, jotting everything down in the small spiral pad he kept in his pocket. When Jesse was finished, Mike went on to ask the usual questions in cases like the one this seemed to be.

He looked at Tania. "Do you have any enemies? Is there anyone who might want to see you permanently out of the way?"

Sasha and Natalya exchanged looks, clearly horrified at the very suggestion, but Tania took the questions in stride.

"No," she answered firmly. "No to both."

Out of the corner of her eye, she caught Jesse watching her. She knew by the expression on his face what he was thinking. He was remembering what she'd told him earlier. A part of her wished she'd never opened up.

She closed her eyes for a second, letting out a long breath. And then she turned to Mike. "There might be someone."

"I'll check it out," Tony volunteered. "Who is it, Tania?"

Tania didn't answer immediately. Instead she looked at her sisters for a long moment. So close that they could read each other's minds at times. She was grateful that neither of them rushed to fill Tony in. That was up to her.

"Jeff Palmer," she finally said. Tony raised an eyebrow in silent query. "Because of me, he was sent to prison."

"No," Natalya cut in firmly. "Because of *him* he was sent to prison," she declared.

Tania waited a moment before clarifying. "He raped

me," she said as simply as possible, allowing none of the pain to come through. She could tell by their reaction that neither man knew about this. Her sisters had kept her secret. "And I went to the police about it. There was a plea bargain and Jeff was sent to jail. He's been out for a few months now," she concluded.

"Is that when you started feeling that someone was watching you?" Mike asked.

She shook her head. "Not immediately." She tried to pinpoint the first time. "Just in the last three weeks, I guess."

Mike had crossed over to the stove and gingerly examined it. He'd pulled a pair of latex gloves out of his pocket and put them on, careful not to smear any evidence.

He glanced at her over his shoulder. "You said all four were turned on?"

It was Jesse who answered. "Yes."

Mike nodded, as if absorbing what was said. "I'll have someone dust for prints." Pulling off the gloves, he crossed back to Tania. "Does anyone else have the key to this apartment?"

Everyone in this room had a key, she thought, except for Jesse. "Just family," Tania answered.

"And you," Natalya interjected, looking at Mike with a whimsical expression on her face.

He gave her a patient, fond look. "I believe you're my alibi."

Tania thought she saw a blush creeping up her sister's face.

"The door wasn't locked when she came home," Jesse suddenly recalled. The two couples turned to look at him, surprised by this new piece of information. "We went to the theater and when we came back, the door wasn't locked."

Natalya spread her hands in protest. "Don't look at me, I locked it when I left—and I left after Kady." The import of her words sank in. Her eyes shifted toward Sasha. "So, unless you dropped by in the interim…"

"Not me," Sasha told her. "I was at the hospital until an hour ago. Mrs. Cassidy *finally* gave birth after four false starts."

Some of the pieces were coming together and it was apparent that Tony didn't like the picture they were forming. "So whoever it was let themselves in to check out the place might have even been here when you came home."

Jesse was quick to set him straight. "I checked out every room, every closet. So unless it was a homicidal monkey hiding in the medicine cabinet, there was no one here when we came in."

"Then they came to get the lay of the land," Mike guessed. "And came back later to tamper with the stove." He turned to Natalya. "You're coming back home with me."

In union there is strength, Jesse thought as he addressed Tania. "That's exactly what I was going to say to you."

Tania gave him a wide-eyed, innocent look. "You want me to go home with Mike? Three's a crowd."

Natalya laughed sympathetically. "Personally, I don't know how you put up with that," she teased. "As for you," she addressed Mike, "since I'm here, I might as well stay here. I'm due at the hospital in less than seven hours and this is closer." She smiled at Tania. "I'll keep Tania company."

Mike seemed a little exasperated, but he knew that tone. There was no arguing with her.

"It's a stubborn family," Tony told him.

Mike sighed, shaking his head. "Tell me something I don't know." He was not about to leave Natalya in a place whose security had been compromised. "Looks like I'll be here for a while."

With that, he took out his cell phone to call someone in the crime scene unit who owed him a favor.

Chapter 14

Over the course of the next week and a half, Jesse saw Tania as often as their two schedules permitted. Because he was working against a deadline, he would bring his blueprints and sketches with him and spend evenings working at her apartment when he couldn't talk her into coming to his. In either situation, he made it a point to pick her up from the hospital no matter how late she got off.

Despite all her efforts to remain nonchalant, Tania quickly grew accustomed to seeing Jesse in the E.R. lobby, waiting for her.

"You know, you really don't have to play my bodyguard."

Sitting on a worn, creased brown vinyl sofa, with a rerun of some program droning on in the background, Jesse discovered to his embarrassment that he had dozed off. The sound of Tania's voice, low and breathy as she'd whispered in his ear, instantly roused him. And aroused him.

Jesse took a deep breath, pulling himself together as best he could. He saw her smile in amusement. "What do you mean 'play'?" he asked. "I thought I was doing a pretty good job of being the real thing."

Actually, he was. He was quickly becoming her knight in shining armor and everyone knew that knights in shining armor weren't real. They belonged in fairy tales. Thinking of him that way only set her up for a fall.

"You don't have to be the real thing, either," she said as he tucked his sketches away and closed his portfolio. "At this rate, you're going to wear out in a couple of days and then who am I going to ask to Natalya's wedding?"

Jesse rose to his feet, his eyebrows momentarily raised in surprise. He was aware of the wedding, but this was the first he'd heard of an invitation. More progress, he thought.

"I won't wear out," he promised, walking beside her to the front entrance. He stepped back, letting her out first. The electronic doors slid open and the night air, pregnant with unshed rain and oppressive humidity, instantly met them, providing a startling contrast to the air-conditioned interior. "You keep these hours and you haven't worn out yet," he pointed out.

"I keep these hours," she agreed, threading her arm through his as they walked to the hospital's parking structure, "but I don't moonlight as an architect." She paused for a moment to brush a kiss to his cheek, surprising him again. "In essence, you're almost juggling two careers. You shouldn't." She saw another protest rise to his lips. "I appreciate what you're doing, Jesse, but really, everything seems to be fine. No one's pushed me off the sidewalk into traffic lately and the stove's been behaving itself." They crossed into the structure and took the stairs down to the basement. "I think I was just being a little paranoid the other week, because I was kind of anxious."

The classic "which came first, the chicken or the egg" runaround, he mused. "That's kind of a catch-22 isn't it?"

"Maybe," she allowed with a casual shrug of her shoulders. Theirs were the only footsteps echoing in the structure on this level. She was secretly glad she wasn't alone. But then, if he weren't here, she'd be waiting for the bus out in the open. It was a trade-off. "If I was anxious about being followed. But that wasn't why I was anxious."

Arriving at his vehicle, Jesse took out his keys and unlocked the passenger side. He held the door open for her. "What was it, then?" he probed.

Tania got in. The moment her body met the seat, she realized how very tired she was—and how grateful she didn't have to wait for public transportation.

She tugged the seat belt into place. "Let's just say I could feel myself heading for a place I hadn't been before and I was afraid it would blow up in my face."

Jesse quickly rounded the rear of his car and got in on the driver's side. "But you don't feel that way anymore?"

That wasn't entirely true. "I've decided to take a wait-and-see stance."

He nodded. The woman was hard to pin down. "Interesting."

"That's one word for it." Jesse closed the door, but made no move to insert the key into the ignition. She eyed him quizzically. Was there something wrong with the car? "Aren't you going to start it?" she asked.

"In a minute."

Before she could ask him what he planned to do in that minute, Tania had her answer. Twisting in his seat, his seat belt still in the at-rest position, Jesse cupped her chin in his hands and kissed her.

Tania had already buckled herself in. Her lips occupied by his, she felt blindly around for the release button and pressed it. As the belt slid back from her body, she moved a breath closer to him. She could feel herself sinking further into the kiss. Without realizing it, she sighed, the outward sign of her vulnerability.

She felt his mouth curving in a smile a second before he drew his head back. "Now I'm ready to go," he told her. Shifting back around, he buckled up and then started the car.

"You certainly are," she murmured. Tania slid the seat belt back into the groove. "Bucket seats do leave something to be desired," she commented. "They sure weren't designed for romance."

He laughed, comically lowering and raising his eyebrows. "Well, there's always the backseat."

Tania did her best to look stern even as his suggestion aroused her. She pointed to the street up ahead. "Just drive," she told him.

"Yes, ma'am." Both hands on the wheel, Jesse guided the car passed the empty guard hut and out onto the street.

Neither one of them saw the figure hiding in the shadows, watching them.

Watching and silently cursing.

* * *

"So, it really wasn't Jeff?" Tania asked her brother-in-law.

Sitting on the arm of the chocolate-colored sofa in her living room, Tony shook his head. It was several days later and Tony, as well as Mike, had devoted as much time to the private investigation as they could. With frustrating results.

"Sorry." He was far from happy with the results. "The fingerprints didn't match. Palmer's are in the system. The prints that were lifted from the knobs on the stove aren't."

He'd had the CSU investigator take samples of all the sisters' prints, using those to pair up with partials that had been found on the knobs and the stove itself. One lone thumbprint did not match any of the sisters. That belonged to the perp, but without matching a set in the system, they were nowhere.

Tania made the best of it. "At least I can stop worrying that Jeff is stalking me." She tried to sound upbeat. This was, after all, an upbeat evening. Leaning forward, she placed her hand on top of his and gave it an appreciative squeeze. "Thanks for looking into that for me."

"We're not out of the woods yet," Tony reminded her. "Someone *did* turn on the gas jets, which means that someone did try to kill you."

She wanted to protest that it might have been one of her sisters that this mysterious "someone" was after, but neither one of them had been pushed into the path of an oncoming bus, nor had either one of them mentioned that they thought someone was following them.

Still, she wanted to release Tony from any sense of

obligation. "There's been nothing for over a week. Maybe whoever it was gave up. Or got hit by a bus," she said whimsically. "At any rate, I'm not going to have this spoil Natalya's wedding."

The doorbell rang and she went to answer it, aware that Tony had risen from the sofa. Ever vigilant, she thought, amused.

"It's just another cop," she announced, stepping away from the doorway and allowing Mike to enter. "She's almost ready," Tania told him as she walked back into the living room.

As if on cue, Natalya came out of her room and into the living room. She looked at her sisters instead of the man she was marrying tomorrow at ten.

"This is my last night as a single woman. Shouldn't I be doing something more decadent than going to the wedding rehearsal?" she asked innocently, struggling to keep a straight face.

"That can be arranged," Mike told her, slipping an arm around her waist and pulling her in close for a quick kiss.

"Not with you." She put her hand on his chest as if to fend him off. "I'm going to be decadent with you for the rest of my life. I was thinking of something else. Maybe a male strip club."

"Stop right there," Sasha warned. "Mama will kill you."

"That'll keep me on the straight and narrow," Natalya commented, nodding.

Sasha merely laughed in response. "First time for everything." Getting up from the sofa, she looked at Tania. "Can we give you a lift to the restaurant?"

Tania shook her head. Bringing a change of clothes with her, Kady was going to the restaurant straight from the hospital. Byron was meeting her there. Their youngest sister and the senior Pulaskis were probably already there. Daddy insisted on being on time, but for the most part, it was a losing battle.

"Jesse is coming by to pick me up in a few minutes." He was actually running a few minutes late, but she kept that to herself.

"We can wait with you," Natalya offered.

"I do not need to be babysat," Tania protested. She glanced at her watch. "Besides, if you don't get to the restaurant soon—" she turned to look at Mike "—Mama is going to think you came to your senses and ran for the hills. She'd come after you."

"Not a chance." Mike looked at Natalya, their own form of silent communication humming between them. "Besides, even if I did make a break for it, my mother would hunt me down before yours ever put on her track shoes."

Natalya laughed, clearly amused. "You obviously don't know my mother."

"Go," Tania urged, putting her hands to Natalya's back and pushing slightly. "All of you. Jesse'll be here in a few minutes and then I'll go."

"Technically," Sasha commented, "since he's not part of the wedding party or the family, Jesse doesn't have to be there." Sasha looked closer at her younger sister. "Unless, of course, he *is* going to become part of the family. Is he, Tania?"

In response, Tania appealed to her brother-in-law. "Tony, please, take your wife and go."

"We live to protect and serve," Tony replied good-naturedly. "Let's go, little mama." Putting his hand to the small of her back, he gently guided her out the door and into the hallway.

Mike was the last one out. Just before he left, he paused for a moment, looking at Tania. "You're sure you don't want one of us to—"

Hands to his arm, she pushed him out the door. Harder than she had her sister.

"I'm sure," she said firmly, then added, "And thank you. But really, Jesse will be here in a couple of minutes. I'll be fine. Really."

Quickly shutting the door behind the groom-to-be, Tania leaned against it for a second and smiled to herself. Natalya was getting a really nice guy. Just as Sasha had. And Kady. All three of her sisters had really lucked out.

Amazing odds in this day and age, she mused, crossing back to the living room.

And what about you? the reflection in the mirror on the wall above the liquor cabinet seemed to ask.

Tania supposed that, when she wasn't being fearful that she was allowing herself to be too trusting again, she just might have blindly stumbled onto something good, as well.

Or someone good.

Because, all things considered, Jesse Steele seemed almost to be too good to be true. She kept waiting for a fatal flaw to surface, for a shoe to drop. For something that would come and burst the bubble that, for now, continued to thrive.

Part of her still felt that maybe she should back away while she still could, before she was hopelessly en-snared and completely lost.

"Who are you kidding?" she asked the wide-eyed woman in the mirror. "There is no more 'before.' You *are* hopelessly ensnared. You *are* completely lost. If this thing ended tomorrow, you'd be devastated and you know it." She stared at her reflection for a long moment. "Face it, Tania," she whispered, "you're in love with the man. The only thing you can do now is hope that he doesn't crush you like a bug."

He didn't seem like the type. On the contrary, everything about him, from the moment she'd met him, fairly shouted "good guy." But even good guys had their dark side, she argued. She had learned that firsthand. Jeff had seemed like a good guy. He hadn't been someone she'd just met casually. She *knew* him.

Or thought she did.

Stop it, Tania ordered herself silently. *You're making yourself crazy.*

Just then, the doorbell rang. Thank God. Jesse. No more internal Ping-Pong matches. With a sense of relief flowing through her, Tania fairly dashed toward the front door, pausing only to slip into her shoes.

"Coming," she cried when the doorbell rang again. She was so focussed on Jesse's arrival, she didn't even look through the peephole the way she normally did. Throwing open the door, she chided, "You realize you're late, don't you?" and then stopped dead.

It wasn't Jesse.

"Not really," the woman in the doorway replied tranquilly. "The way I see it, I'm really just in time."

Tania stared at her, confused. It was the volunteer from the hospital. The one she'd attempted to treat for a bad back. She'd disappeared after being sent to the

X-ray department. Not for the day but ever since then. Tania had asked after her only to be told that the woman was no longer coming in to volunteer.

"Carol?" Tania stood just inside the apartment, blocking the way in. "What are you doing here?"

Slightly taller than Tania and a little wider, the woman entered as if she belonged there. Once inside, she pushed the door closed. "What I'm doing here is stopping you from making a horrible mistake."

"What mistake?" Tania could feel her stomach knotting. There was something wrong with this woman. Why hadn't she seen it before?

The woman's eyes narrowed. "You need to stop seeing Jesse Steele."

Tania could feel her temper flaring. "That isn't any business of yours."

"Oh, yes, it is," the woman answered in a steely voice that, any moment, sounded as if it would cross over into hysteria. "He's my husband."

For a split second, Tania felt her knees go weak. "What?"

A smug, cold smile took over the woman's pretty face. As she spoke, she moved about, as if there was unharnessed energy within her, energy that was liable to explode at any moment. But she made sure she didn't move away from the area of the front door.

"Didn't tell you that, did he? That he was married. That he vowed undying love to me such a short while ago. He's a charmer, that one," she allowed. "I don't blame you for having your head turned." She set her mouth hard. "But now you need to go."

The way she said it sent shivers down Tania's spine.

She refused to show any fear, sensing that the woman would only feel empowered.

"No," Tania declared, "you do." She made a lunge for the doorknob. Blocking her, the other woman pushed Tania aside so hard, she stumbled backward and nearly fell. She caught herself at the last minute, glaring at the intruder.

Just then, the phone began to ring. Tania's head jerked in the direction of the telephone.

"Leave it!" the woman ordered.

From where she stood, she could see the LED display. "It's Jesse," she said. Why was he calling? Why wasn't he here already?

"Let it ring," the woman snarled. Tania went for it anyway. The woman got to her before she could reach the phone and grabbed her by the hair. Tania yelped in pain. The next moment the woman shoved her down on the floor. "I said leave it!" she screamed.

Aching, Tania scrambled to her feet. "What the hell do you want?"

The woman's voice became singsong. "I want to do a good deed," she told her. "I came to warn you." And then her face clouded over, her expression malevolent. "Stay away from Jesse. He's bad news."

"Then why do you want him?" Tania challenged.

"Because he's *my* bad news," the woman all but screamed in her face.

Tania stood her ground, all the while desperately trying to think of a way to overpower the deranged woman and get the upper hand. She wasn't going to be a victim again.

"Look, 'your husband' is going to be here any minute," she retorted nastily. "Maybe you'd like to tell him all this yourself."

Tania was not prepared for the smug expression that came over the woman's face. "No, he's not." Her voice was low, dark. Mocking. "Jesse isn't coming to the rescue this time."

The uneasiness in her stomach began to spread. What had the woman done to Jesse? Had he just called her for help? Called and not gotten an answer because this witch was holding her hostage, threatening her?

"How do you know that?" she demanded.

"I know that because your 'hero' is having car trouble." Smug satisfaction fairly radiated from the woman. "Cars don't run without a distributor cap. It'll take him time to figure out. Time you and I can use well."

And then it suddenly all became clear to her. Why hadn't she thought of this before? "You're Ellen, aren't you?"

The mention of her name made the woman all but preen before her. "So he did tell you about me, after all."

She needed to get Ellen frustrated. To get her confused so that she let her guard down. "Just that you were some sick, twisted woman who'd been stalking him."

Fury entered Ellen's eyes. She looked really crazy, Tania thought. "I didn't stalk him! I'm his wife!" she insisted. "Wives are *supposed* to be around their husbands!" She held up her left hand, waving her ring finger in the air. "See? A wedding ring." She all but thrust it into Tania's face. "We're married, you bitch, and it's time that you stepped out of the picture once and for all. Now, let's go."

But Tania didn't make a move. Someone at the restaurant would realize she wasn't there and come back for her. All she had to do was hang on until then. "I'm not going anywhere with you."

"Oh, yes, you are."

She never even saw the taser until it was too late. One scream and Tania crumpled to the floor, unconscious.

"Oh, yes, you are," Ellen repeated triumphantly.

Chapter 15

Jesse admittedly knew very little about cars beyond keeping the gas tank filled and bringing it in for regular oil changes and maintenance. Other than adding oil once in a while and keeping jumper cables in the trunk, just in case his battery died, what went on beneath the hood was a complete mystery to him.

In exchange for regular maintenance, his present vehicle gave him no grief. So when he got in behind the wheel after stopping at his apartment to change, and heard absolutely nothing when he turned the key in the ignition, Jesse was caught entirely off guard.

Mystification swiftly became a hazy, uneasy feeling he couldn't quantify or put his finger on. Hoping it was some kind of fluke, Jesse turned the key again. Without success. The vehicle stubbornly maintained its silence.

Cursing the fact that his car should pick now of all

times to become uncooperative, he popped the hood release just to the left of the steering column and got out. Jesse lifted the hood and immediately found himself staring into no-man's-land.

He had no idea what he was searching for. He just knew he needed the car resurrected. And fast.

As Jesse tried to decide his next move, the stock broker who lived across the hall from him pulled into his parking spot several spaces down. Getting out of his own car, Evan, who'd been kidding him good-naturedly about his newfound fame as New York's current reigning hero, called out a greeting.

"Hi, Hero. Trouble?"

"You might say that." Jesse felt his frustration mounting. "I drove it here less than an hour ago and now it suddenly won't start."

Curious, Evan crossed over to him and looked over his shoulder into the Honda's yawning mouth.

"It sure as hell won't," he agreed. "Not without a distributor cap."

Jesse looked at him blankly. "A what?"

Evan pointed to where the distributor cap should have been in this car. "Little thing that the spark plugs take their orders from so that the engine fires correctly. You don't have one."

Jesse frowned. "Is that normal?"

"No, that most certainly isn't. Cars don't run without distributor caps." Evan came to his own conclusion. "Someone's playing a joke on you. Either that, or they have it in for you."

The uneasy feeling increased. Something was wrong, very wrong. He immediately thought of Tania.

"Evan, can I borrow your car?" he asked, turning to his neighbor. "I wouldn't ask, but I've got a feeling that it just might be a matter of life or death."

Evan dug into his pocket. "You heroes always this dramatic?" he asked with a laugh, taking his car key off his key ring. He held it out to Jesse.

"Only when the situation calls for it. Thanks." Key in hand, Jesse hurried over to Evan's sports car. Getting in, he put the key into the ignition and the engine purred to life. "I'll fill the tank up for you," he promised.

Jesse's restless irritation continued to grow as he drove. Despite weaving in and out of traffic in an attempt to gain headway, he wasn't making the kind of progress he wanted to. The minutes were moving as fast as the traffic was not. For a moment he even toyed with the idea of driving on the sidewalk, the way they did in the movies. But the sidewalks were even more crowded than the streets were.

Running a red light, Jesse actually hoped that there was a policeman around to pull him over. Sirens would clear the way for him once he explained why he was rushing. But he made it through the intersection without incident. The only thing he attracted was a barrage of curses from the other drivers.

Maybe he was overreacting. Flipping open his cell phone, he called Tania on the house line. If she answered, he'd tell her that he was running late. Hearing her voice would put this prickly uneasiness to rest.

The phone rang five times and then went to her answering machine.

Maybe she was already on her way to the restaurant. Hoping against hope, he tried her cell phone. With the same results. The knots in his stomach tightened.

This wasn't good.

When he finally arrived at her building, Jesse left the car parked right before the main entrance, an area clearly marked as a no parking zone.

With luck, they'd both be out before anyone had a chance to write him up. If she was home.

The elevator was elsewhere in the building. He wasn't about to wait. Jesse took the stairs. Adrenaline roared through his veins when he got to her door. Rather than ring her doorbell, he used the key Tania had given him just yesterday. It struck him as ironic that at the time he'd told her he didn't need a key because he wouldn't be coming over when she wasn't already there.

Please be here.

Unlocking the door, Jesse held his breath as he walked in. "Tania? Tania, are you home?"

He called her name over and over as he strode through the apartment, looking from one room to another. She was nowhere to be found.

Frustrated, he called her cell phone again. As it rang in his ear, he heard ringing coming from somewhere within the room. Tracking the sound, he found that it was coming from the hall closet.

Jesse threw the door open and discovered the ringing came from her purse. The purse was hanging from a hook inside the closet. Tania would have never left her purse behind.

Now it was official. Something was wrong.

His next call was to Tony. The moment he heard the phone being answered, he started talking. "Tony, this is Jesse. Don't repeat anything I say, just listen. I don't want to upset her family. Is Tania there?"

"No." Tony lowered his voice and could only hope that the detective had withdrawn from the others in order to talk more freely. "We left her at the apartment, waiting for you."

"She's not here." Jesse dragged his hand through his hair, trying to think. "Her purse is here, but she's not. Hold it," Jesse said, suddenly becoming aware of something.

Lowering the phone away from his ear, he took a deep breath. And then another one. There was a scent in the air, a very specific scent.

A scent he recognized.

Oh, God, how could he have been so stupid?

He quickly put the phone against his ear again. "Tony, I think Tania's been kidnapped and I know who has her."

"Palmer had an alibi," Tony reminded him. "But it wasn't airtight. I'm going to—"

"It's not Palmer," Jesse cut in. "It's not about Tania. This is about me." The admission alone made him almost physically ill.

"You? What are you talking about?" Tony wanted to know.

He didn't have time to go into detail, but he gave the other man just the bare bones. "About a year ago, I was being stalked by this woman from work. She had a few screws loose. Management fired her. I thought that it was all over six months ago."

There was no emotion in the voice on the other end. Tony required facts. "What makes you think it isn't?"

"The woman used to wear this one particular perfume. It had an almost sickeningly sweet scent. I'm catching a whiff of it in Tania's apartment."

"Give me the woman's name," Tony instructed. "I'm going to call this in and I'll be right there."

"Her name's Ellen Sederholm." To be on the safe side, Jesse spelled it out for him.

"Got it. Sit tight," Tony ordered. The line went dead.

He couldn't sit tight. He couldn't sit at all.

This was all his fault, Jesse thought, pacing restlessly. He'd been so focused on Tania's pain after she'd told him about the date rape, it never occurred to him that Ellen might have come out of the woodwork to stalk him again. The woman was crazy. If she'd seen him with Tania…

He didn't want to go there.

But he had to go somewhere, do something. Jesse clenched and unclenched his hands impotently at his sides. Every minute that went by was a minute Tania might not have to spare. But what could he—

Jesse stopped pacing. He saw Natalya's laptop on the coffee table. It was open. He sank onto the sofa. The laptop was still on.

Hitting a key, he watched the screensaver slowly vanish. A Web site came on. Natalya was still logged on to the Internet.

Bless you, Natalya.

Opening up a search engine he was familiar with, Jesse pulled up what served as the white pages. He typed in Ellen's name and then specified the city and state.

Three choices popped up. He vaguely remembered Ellen telling him that she'd been named after someone in her family. "I'm the new, improved Ellen Sederholm," she'd told him.

The first Ellen Sederholm lived in Staten Island. The

second was located all the way out in Wantagh. That was out on Long Island.

The third lived two blocks away.

That had to be the one.

Jesse scribbled down the address and phone number on a napkin that was on the coffee table. Shoving it into his pocket, Jesse left the apartment and ran down all five flights to the ground level.

He didn't bother getting into Evan's car. He could run the distance faster than he could drive. The fact that the vehicle stood a good chance of being ticketed and towed away was something he couldn't stop to deal with right now.

The only thing on his mind was Tania and this nagging feeling that he might already be too late.

Tania came to.

She was lying on something cool and hard. A roach skittered by inches from her face and she gasped.

Or tried to.

There was tape over her mouth. Her wrists were bound behind her, and she pulled so hard she thought her shoulder would pop. Her ankles were taped, as well.

Fear slithered through her.

"You woke up. Too bad," Ellen said. She knelt beside her, a roll of duct tape in her hands. "I was hoping that you'd stay unconscious until I finished gift-wrapping you." The laugh that followed was chilling. "It would have been better that way for both of us."

Tania began to buck and wriggle, trying to get free.

Ellen reached for the taser, her eyes malevolent. "Don't make me use this again," she warned.

Tania stopped moving.

* * *

Jesse ran all the way to Ellen's building. He took the six concrete steps leading to the front door two at a time. A small, elderly woman unlocked the wrought-iron door leading into the building. It was his way in.

"Let me get that for you," he offered.

The woman smiled her thanks and didn't challenge his presence. "Thank you, young man. Are you new here? I'm Margaret Gallagher. I like to meet the new people," she told him as she entered the foyer ahead of him. "Been here going on thirty years. Seen so many come and go."

Jesse was about to start hunting for Ellen's apartment number. There was a wall of mailboxes on the far side of the foyer, some with apartment numbers beside the names, some not.

He crossed his fingers mentally as he looked at the woman.

"Do you know an Ellen Sederholm?"

The woman instantly beamed, a squadron of wrinkles appearing at both sides of her mouth. "Yes, I do. Lovely girl. Talks about her husband all the time, although I've never met him. Jesse is his name. Always thought that was a girl's name," Margaret told him.

Ellen was fantasizing about him as her husband. He tried not to think about how far gone she had to be. Or how dangerous. He was positive now that she had to be the one behind the gas leak.

"Would you know her apartment number, Mrs. Gallagher?" In order to coax her, he added, "I'm an old friend of Ellen's from college."

"Oh, she'll like that. She lives in apartment 6-D." Jesse

started up the stairs. "But I don't think you'll find her there," she called after him. He stopped and turned around to look at her. "I saw her going down to the basement a little while ago. She had a friend with her. Poor thing was leaning all over her. Looked rather peaked."

That had to be Tania. He couldn't picture her submitting willingly. Had Ellen drugged her? "What's in the basement?" he asked Mr. Gallagher.

"Storage spaces." She sighed. "Mine's so full I'm going to have to go through it someday, start throwing things out. Hard to part with memories," she murmured. "Well, here's the elevator."

Jesse sailed down the stairs. He was at the elderly woman's side in an instant, just as the elevator door opened.

"Would you mind if I go down to the basement first?" Not waiting for Margaret's answer, he reached over to the row of buttons and pressed "B."

The woman scrutinized him. "Awfully anxious to see her, aren't you?"

He faced forward as the door closed again. "It's been a long time."

"Well, take my advice and don't let her husband get the wrong idea," she chuckled. "Ellen says he's very jealous of her."

They'd reached the basement. Jesse's blood ran cold. Getting out, he paused, his hand on the door, keeping it from closing again. "Are the storage spaces arranged in any order?"

"How clever of you," Margaret beamed. "First row, first floor, second row, second floor, and so on. I'm

3-C," she told him. "Come by and visit me sometime. I love to talk to young people."

Jesse drew back his hand. The door began to close. "I'll do that," he promised, already turning away.

The basement smelled musty and the artificial overhead illumination was of a low wattage, casting a mournful light about the area.

Remembering what Margaret had said, Jesse counted off five rows, then stopped at the sixth. There were ten compartments, all with their doors shut. The numbers on them meant nothing to him. He began to try the doors one by one.

The first five were locked. Approaching the sixth, he saw the light seeping out from beneath the door. Had someone left it on, or was there someone inside?

Holding his breath, he turned the knob, and it gave. Heart pounding, Jesse opened the door very slowly, praying it wouldn't creak and give him away.

The storage area was filled with boxes piled on top of each other, forming towers taller than he was. Jesse inched his way in, careful not to knock over any of the boxes. His eyes grew accustomed to the poor lighting.

And then he saw her.

Ellen.

Her back was to him. On her knees, she was busy ripping a length of silver duct tape from an all but depleted roll. She was wrapping something.

And then, to his horror, he realized it wasn't something, it was someone.

Tania.

Tania was bound with duct tape. Not just her mouth, hands and feet, but her chest, her stomach, her throat.

It looked as if Ellen was intent on wrapping *all* of her, including her face.

"Ellen," he said sharply, "get away from her."

Ellen wasn't startled. She didn't even turn around to look at him. Instead she continued pulling another length of tape from the roll.

"I knew you'd come back to me," she told him in a singsong voice. "Knew you'd realize that you missed me. That we belonged together. I made it easy for you to find me."

"Get away from her, Ellen," he retorted. When she went on tearing the length of tape off the roll, he pushed her aside. Dropping to his knees, he grabbed an end and began ripping away the duct tape. Tania winced, but there was relief in her eyes.

"She's evil," Ellen cried, her calmness shattering like a fragile spider's web. She tried to pull him away, but couldn't. "Don't you see?" she screamed. "She turned you against me. We belong together. You love *me,* not her. She cast some kind of a spell over you, that's why I have to get rid of her," she cried frantically. "To save you. Stop it!" Ellen beat on his back, trying to get him to stop removing the duct tape.

He didn't waste time looking at her. "Ellen, you need help. I promise I'll see that you get it, people who'll help you," he said as he quickly pulled off strip after strip. "I'm sorry, this is going to really hurt," he told Tania just before he yanked away the strip over her mouth.

"Jesse, look out," Tania cried.

Jesse turned just in time to see the taser coming at him. He ducked, then moving quickly, he grabbed Ellen's wrist and twisted it.

Ellen shrieked like a wounded animal as the taser hit her chest. And then she slid bonelessly to the concrete floor, unconscious.

Losing no time, Jesse tore off two strips of the remaining duct tape, using one to bind her hands, the other to bind her feet. Secure that Ellen no longer posed an immediate threat, he resumed removing the tape from Tania's body.

She sat up, working with him. "Look at the back wall," she told him.

Turning, Jesse looked and then his mouth dropped open. The wall was covered with photographs of him, some garnered from various newspapers, the rest digital photographs that Ellen had to have taken herself while stalking him.

"Damn," he muttered incredulously under his breath.

"That's one hell of a groupie you have there, Jesse," Tania said, pulling off the last of the tape. Throwing it aside, she took in a deep breath to calm herself. It was over, thank God. Over. "She was just going to leave me down here to die, like some giant caterpillar in a duct tape cocoon."

"I'm sorry, baby, I'm so sorry," he said over and over again.

Tania threw her arms around him. "Sorry? You saved me." She buried her face against his chest. "I knew you'd come for me, I just knew it." Lifting her head, she looked at him as she blinked back tears. A half smile played on her lips. "I knew you couldn't resist playing a hero again."

"Are you all right?" he asked her. His eyes swept over her face, her body, to assure himself that she was in one piece. "Did she hurt you?"

Tania tried to muster a smile. "Well, the taser was no picnic, but otherwise, I'm okay." She blew out a long, emotional breath. "Boy, loving you has some really heavy consequences, doesn't it?"

For the second time in as many minutes, his mouth dropped open. "Loving me?" he repeated, stunned. "You love me?"

She caught her lip between her teeth. Okay, she blew it. The man just had a stalker after him. A pushy woman was the last thing he'd welcome. "Wasn't supposed to say that, was I? Sorry, it was an emotional minute."

She continued talking, trying to backpedal. Jesse wasn't listening. Instead he framed her face with his hands and looked at her, looked at what he had almost lost. It made his head spin.

Cutting through the flow of her rhetoric, he said, "I love you."

Tania stopped talking. And then he saw a smile enter her eyes. "Really."

"Really." He said it as if it was an oath. Because it was. An oath and a pledge. He intended to love her as long as he lived. As long as *he* lived.

The rush of joy that surged through her almost made Tania dizzy. It took her a long moment to get her bearings.

"Okay," she said slowly, "I can live with that."

He grinned. "Can you live with being my wife?"

The brightness of her smile made up for the dim illumination in the storage area.

"Even better." And then her eyebrows rose a little as a grain of skepticism entered. "You're not just saying that because your groupie there almost turned me into a silver doorstop—"

"Shut up," Jesse told her, bringing his mouth down on hers.

"Just like a hero, throwing his weight around," she murmured.

Jesse tasted Tania's smile on his lips just before he deepened his kiss.

The sound of approaching sirens echoed in the background.

It looked like he was going to be paying Isaac Epstein a visit in the near future after all. As he recalled, the man had some beautiful diamonds. One would make a perfect engagement ring for the perfect woman, Jesse thought, just before he stopped thinking at all.

* * * * *

Enjoy a sneak preview of
MATCHMAKING WITH A MISSION
by B.J. Daniels,
part of the **WHITEHORSE, MONTANA** *miniseries.*
Available from Harlequin Intrigue
in April 2008.

Nate Dempsey has returned to Whitehorse to uncover the truth about his past...

Nate sensed someone watching the house and looked out in surprise to see a woman astride a paint horse just on the other side of the fence. He quickly stepped back from the filthy second-floor window, although he doubted she could have seen him. Only a little of the June sun pierced the dirty glass to glow on the dust-coated floor at his feet as he waited a few heartbeats before he looked out again.

The place was so isolated he hadn't expected to see another soul. Like the front yard, the dirt road was waist-high with weeds. When he'd broken the lock on the back door, he'd had to kick aside a pile of rotten leaves that had blown in from last fall.

As he sneaked a look, he saw that she was still there, staring at the house in a way that unnerved him. He shielded his eyes from the glare of the sun off the dirty window and studied her, taking in her head of long blond hair that feathered out in the breeze from under her Western straw hat.

She wore a tan canvas jacket, jeans and boots. But it was the way she sat astride the brown-and-white horse that nudged the memory.

He felt a chill as he realized he'd seen her before. In that very spot. She'd been just a kid then. A kid on a pretty paint horse. Not this one—the markings were different. Anyway, it couldn't have been the same horse, considering the last time he had seen her was more than twenty years ago. That horse would be dead by now.

His mind argued it probably wasn't even the same girl. But he knew better. It was the way she sat the horse, so at home in a saddle and secure in her world on the other side of that fence.

To the boy he'd been, she and her horse had represented freedom, a freedom he'd known he would never have—even after he escaped this house.

Nate saw her shift in the saddle, and for a moment he feared she planned to dismount and come toward the house. With Ellis Harper in his grave, there would be little to keep her away.

To his relief, she reined her horse around and rode back the way she'd come.

As he watched her ride away, he thought about the way she'd stared at the house—today and years ago. While the smartest thing she could do was to stay clear of this house, he had a feeling she'd be back.

Finding out her name should prove easy, since he figured she must live close by. As for her interest in Harper House… He would just have to make sure it didn't become a problem.

* * * * *

Be sure to look for
MATCHMAKING WITH A MISSION
and other suspenseful Harlequin Intrigue stories,
available in April
wherever books are sold.

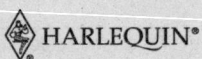

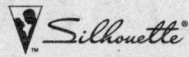

SPECIAL EDITION™

Introducing a brand-new miniseries

Men of
Mercy Medical

Gabe Thorne moved to Las Vegas to open a
new branch of his booming construction
business—and escape from a recent tragedy.
But when his teenage sister showed up pregnant
on his doorstep, he really had his hands full.
Luckily, in turning to Dr. Rebecca Hamilton for
the medical care his sister needed, he found
a cure for himself....

Starting with

THE MILLIONAIRE
AND THE M.D.

by *TERESA SOUTHWICK,*

available in April wherever books are sold.

REQUEST YOUR FREE BOOKS!

2 FREE NOVELS PLUS 2 FREE GIFTS!

Silhouette® Romantic

SUSPENSE

Sparked by Danger, Fueled by Passion!

YES! Please send me 2 FREE Silhouette® Romantic Suspense novels and my 2 FREE gifts (gifts are worth about $10). After receiving them, if I don't wish to receive any more books, I can return the shipping statement marked "cancel." If I don't cancel, I will receive 4 brand-new novels every month and be billed just $4.24 per book in the U.S. or $4.99 per book in Canada, plus 25¢ shipping and handling per book plus applicable taxes, if any*. That's a savings of at least 15% off the cover price! I understand that accepting the 2 free books and gifts places me under no obligation to buy anything. I can always return a shipment and cancel at any time. Even if I never buy another book from Silhouette, the two free books and gifts are mine to keep forever.

240 SDN EEX6 340 SDN EEYJ

Name	(PLEASE PRINT)	
Address		Apt. #
City	State/Prov.	Zip/Postal Code

Signature (if under 18, a parent or guardian must sign)

Mail to the **Silhouette Reader Service:**

IN U.S.A.: P.O. Box 1867, Buffalo, NY 14240-1867
IN CANADA: P.O. Box 609, Fort Erie, Ontario L2A 5X3

Not valid to current subscribers of Silhouette Romantic Suspense books.

Want to try two free books from another line?
Call 1-800-873-8635 or visit www.morefreebooks.com.

* Terms and prices subject to change without notice. N.Y. residents add applicable sales tax. Canadian residents will be charged applicable provincial taxes and GST. This offer is limited to one order per household. All orders subject to approval. Credit or debit balances in a customer's account(s) may be offset by any other outstanding balance owed by or to the customer. Please allow 4 to 6 weeks for delivery. Offer available while quantities last.

Your Privacy: Silhouette is committed to protecting your privacy. Our Privacy Policy is available online at www.eHarlequin.com or upon request from the Reader Service. From time to time we make our lists of customers available to reputable third parties who may have a product or service of interest to you. If you would prefer we not share your name and address, please check here. ☐

SRS08

nocturne™

The Bloodrunners
trilogy continues with book #2.

The hunt meant more to Jeremy Burns than dominance—it meant facing the woman he left behind. Once Jillian Murphy had belonged to Jeremy, but now she was the Spirit Walker to the Silvercrest wolves. It would take more than the rights of nature for Jeremy to renew his claim on her—and she would not go easily once he had.

LAST WOLF HUNTING

by RHYANNON BYRD

Available in April wherever books are sold.

Be sure to watch out for the last book,
Last Wolf Watching, available in May.

Silhouette®
Romantic
SUSPENSE

COMING NEXT MONTH

#1507 DANGER SIGNALS—Kathleen Creighton
The Taken

Detective Wade Callahan is determined to discover the killer in a string of unsolved murders—without the help of his new partner. Tierney Doyle is used to being criticized for her supposed psychic abilities, but even the tough-as-nails—and drop-dead-gorgeous—detective can't deny what she has uncovered. And Tierney is slowly discovering that working so closely to Wade could be lethal.

#1508 A HERO TO COUNT ON—Linda Turner
Broken Arrow Ranch

Katherine Wyatt would never trust a man again, until she was forced to trust the sexy stranger at her family's ranch. Undercover investigator Hunter Sinclair wasn't looking to get romantically involved, especially with Katherine. But when she started dating a potential suspect, he had no choice but to let her in…and risk losing his heart.

#1509 THE DARK SIDE OF NIGHT—Cindy Dees
H.O.T. Watch

Fleeing for his life, secret agent Mitch Perovski is given permission to use the senator's boat as an out…but he didn't think he'd have the senator's daughter to accompany him. Kinsey Hollingsworth just wanted to escape the scandal she was mixed up in. Now she's thrown into a game of cat and mouse and her only chance for survival is Mitch. Can she withstand their burning attraction long enough to stay alive?

#1510 LETHAL ATTRACTION—Diana Duncan
Forever in a Day

When Sabrina Matthews is held at gunpoint, the last person she expects to save her life was SWAT pilot—and ex-crush—Grady O'Rourke. Grady is shocked when he receives a call informing him his next mission is to protect Sabrina. Though Grady is confident in his skills, she is the only woman who can get under his skin. He may be in greater danger of losing his heart than his life.